RYAN E

Jodi and Mike —

Leave room for mystery in
your life!

Love,

Ryan Elaindcan

Beneath
the Trees

Beneath the Trees

ISBN-13: 978-0-9978458-2-2
LCCN: 2016917985

glassblowerscat.com

For Sally

Author's Note

If there is a place where I find it easiest to believe in the existence of a reality beyond our own, it is deep in the woods. Trees—the older, mossier, and more weathered, the better—wall off our mundanity with old magic, dredged up from the soil, that we can longer harness but which tingles the dark edges of our collective memory. Some part of us still remembers, from ages long past, that we used to believe every tree and river and stone housed a spirit, one we could enrage, or appease, or supplicate, if we were wise enough—or foolish enough—to meet it on the borders. And I think that some part of us (maybe a bigger part, or maybe a smaller part) knows just how true and how false those old beliefs were, and longs for a certainty lost to our own enlightenment. To successfully lose oneself amidst the trees, far from sight or sound of our own world, is to stand on the precipice of that certainty, to feel the faint updraft of it on our faces, stirring the cobwebs clustered in the corners of what we now call imagination.

Even at this late hour, when we in the developed world have been driving back the forests for decades—hemming them in, taming them, sanitizing them—the smallest patch of trees along the highway can still call out to me as I go zipping past in my cocoon of metal and wheels. For a few moments I will be elsewhere, listening to the whispers of the leaves as they make the sun dance for its survival on the ground at my feet. One cold February morning, on my way to a far less magical destination, my eyes landed on a small outpost of bare branches against the sky, a few hundred feet behind an old barn, and something crawled its way out from between the gray, frost-bitten trunks and into what I call my imagination: something old, and almost worn out, but not quite ready to fade away from this world for good.

So I have tried to breathe a little life back into it, and if I have succeeded, you will know it when next you stand amidst the trees and feel that faint tingle of certainty beneath the surface of your mind.

RYAN ELAINSKA

Beneath the Trees

1

I should have known better than to go running in the woods after dark like that. But I just had to escape. The house felt like a cage to me, with Molly sleeping most of the day—they'd said she would start doing that, toward the end. And even when she was awake, I could barely see *her* in her eyes, like she'd already gone. It was almost better when she was sleeping, except that then I was supposed to be writing—and that was going nowhere. Whenever I sat down at the piano, whenever I tried to clear out my mind and let the song assemble itself at the tips of my fingers, that's when all the stored-up thoughts of the day would come rushing in. Everything I'd been keeping at bay by cleaning and making food and taking care of those final pieces of business that made those last few days of her life feel like signing a mortgage—it would all find me then, and the music would fly away.

That was the night I cracked. Molly had fallen asleep after lunch—not that she ate much—and I knew she wouldn't wake up for a long time yet. I could risk not being there for one of those few minutes of consciousness. The moon was bright enough, I thought, that I wouldn't get lost, even out in the woods.

At first it felt good: just the relief of using my body to do anything at all that fulfilled its purpose, and the freedom of the whole open world around me. The forest welcomed me back in—seemed to know I just needed its presence and silence: just to be, and to not think. I turned off the path almost right away, and the outstretched branches brushing against me on either side felt like hands reaching out to reassure me, to tell me I was still in my right place. The moon-shadow on the ground, running along ahead of me, never letting me catch up to it, looked so free and wild as it flickered and twisted on the fallen branches and leaves that I could almost pretend I wasn't holding it down, keeping it anchored to a reality it so clearly longed to escape. If I could have freed it then—just let it scamper away into the night on its own—would it have found a new shape? Or would it have disintegrated after a few steps—lost any life of its own without me to give it shape or purpose?

I was running wherever my feet and my shadow took me at first, but as I strayed farther and farther from the path I came to places where the trees began to seem strange. Maybe I would have recognized their shapes in the daylight, but by night they only reminded me that I was now far from home. Home: where Molly might be waking up by now, wondering where I was, why I was not at least by her side for as long as I could be, while she slowly wandered out into a different kind of darkness.

I was just about to stop and turn around, to run straight home again, when far ahead and to the left, out of the shadows of two huge oaks that stood side-by-side in the darkness, a tall shape passed across the edge of my sight. It brought me to a halt at once. I tried to peer into the darkness, but at first I could only see the trees and their skeletons on the ground, moving gently in the wind. Then, just as I was about to turn toward home, the figure moved again, unmistakeable even in the witchery of the moonlight.

If we had bears in our part of the country, I could have convinced myself it was a bear. It towered up into the sky, a black shape against the starlight, at least twelve feet high, but it moved like a human—or some nightmare mutation of one. Its legs were too thick, and its head, perched on wide, misshapen shoulders, was too small, and the flash of its arms as they swung nearly to the ground showed long fingers almost like claws.

I wanted to turn and run for home, as I had been meaning to do already, but at the sight of this creature my blood froze in my veins. I could hear my own breath rattling across the stillness of the forest, ragged and short, and my mind went blank. But not with fear. It wasn't fear, not like it was just a wild animal that had cornered me in the forest by night, far from home. I knew that feeling, but this was something more—more than mortal terror—more like the dread of the darkness itself, the true darkness we see when we look into the unknown.

The sky was turning gray, clouds coming up from the west on a gathering wind. Even my shadow fled away from me as the clouds blotted out the light of the moon, and there I was, rooted to the ground alone. The giant in the shadows, and me.

A deep breath: that's what I need, I think. So I force myself to take it. The monster hasn't moved again, and maybe it hasn't seen me. Or maybe it isn't real. I've imagined it, and a deep breath will calm me down and drive away the terror of the night. It did—enough to unfreeze my legs so I could start to back away from the creature in the trees. I take a few backward steps, then turn all in a flash and start to run, back toward home, toward the lights of the kitchen shining out to me across the field beyond the trees, toward Molly and the comfort of her narrow hands clasped in mine as she sleeps.

Without my shadow to lead me, I realize I have no idea which way takes me home. I stop again and cast a glance over my shoulder. Nothing. Nothing but the darkness behind me. Darkness, and silence. The creature in the shadows isn't following me—or so I tell myself. I glance around, then try to reorient my sense of direction. I take off running again, a little to the left, but still that fear nags at the back of my mind, that I'm only heading farther into the woods—farther away from home. Even though I know the folly in it, I take another quarter-turn back to the right.

All of a sudden, out of the darkness just ahead, that same monstrous shape appears, striding across my path. It shudders as it turns—turns to look at me, I know. I halt in my tracks, and now I'm really afraid. My heart was already pounding, but now it's in my throat, and that's all that stops me screaming. The monster takes a step toward me… then another. I try to back away, but my feet won't take orders from me anymore. The huge shape looms over me—a shadowy caricature of a human being—and I see one of its clawed hands reaching out for me.

Then I go blind—blind with a light that flares up out of the darkness. It sears away my vision, and for a second I'm too confused to be afraid. I cover my eyes and twist away from the light, and I hear a sound like a snarl—short and guttural, like a disappointed predator. A heavy, rustling series of footsteps retreats away from me, and I turn around again, shielding my eyes.

2

Above my head, beyond where the monster had been standing, a ball of fire hangs in the air. Green flames —not yellow or orange—burn away the darkness and dread about me. At first I can only stare until my eyes burn in my head and I have to raise my hand again to block the light. Then I see the trees: familiar trees, trees I could place at any time of day or night. I turn to look over my shoulder, now realizing that home lies behind me. Then I look at the green fire again.

It only hovers above the ground, keeping back the night, as if its sole purpose were to show me the way home. I take a step toward it, almost against my own will (even though I no longer feel afraid), and for a half-second I think I see a face looking out at me from inside the burning orb. But it flares brighter again, then begins to rise, out of reach of my hands and my curiosity. It floats past me, along the line that will take me back to the path, then home. My heart is still racing, but I take the hint and stumble into a run again.

I'd seen that green flame before, once, a few weeks before that night. Molly had insisted that she had enough energy to go out into the woods after dinner, to watch the sunset. She was already getting weak, then, but she was still herself, and not quite ready to give up all our rituals. I made her put on a sweater, and we held hands as we walked past the barn, out into the field behind the house, watching the dying sun turn the half-bare branches of the trees orange and red.

We took our time; I made sure to stop every few minutes and pretend I wanted to examine a sapling or some wildflowers so Molly could stand still and catch her breath.

"I know what you're doing," she said, after I'd done this two times.

I replied with just an "Mmmmmm?" and picked a violet to stick behind her ear. It popped nicely against her blond hair, and I couldn't resist kissing her temple, just above where her cheekbones were already beginning to show a little more starkly as she lost weight.

She said, "I'm a reasonable, adult woman; you can just ask me if I want to rest."

"Do you want to rest?" I asked.

"Nice," she said.

She took my hand, and we walked on into the trees. I kept glancing over at her to see how the violet looked, and she would smile but pretend not to notice otherwise.

The leaves were just starting to sprout on most of the trees, and the sun shone through above, making everything warm and soft-shadowed down on the forest floor. The path that someone had trod through the forest long before Molly and I settled there gave us plenty of flat, even ground, and I scuffed through the winter's decay of leaves, kicking some of them up into the air every now and then, and making Molly laugh and jab me in the ribs with her elbow every time.

After the third or fourth time, she said, "I love it when you're a kid."

And I said, "Who says this is only for kids?"

"It's the delight," she said. "Everything is so magical to you."

"Not everything," I said. But she was right about that one thing.

Our favorite place is—was—near the far edge of the forest, where you could almost, but not quite, see the other side. A few months after we moved in, a huge old tree had fallen, in just the right place to sit and look west. We turned off the path toward it and started pushing our way through the new shoots and fallen branches, and Molly slid her hand up to hold me by the upper arm as we walked.

Just before you get to the old tree, there's a huge walnut tree—I mean a really massive one—standing off to the right in a tiny clearing, with a nearly perfect circle of trees around it. They aren't spaced evenly, so it doesn't look exactly like someone planted them this way on purpose, but I like to believe it was meant to happen. Molly slowed down a little as we passed by the clearing, looking up at the big walnut tree.

"Do you need to rest?" I asked.

And she said, "No," softly, as though only part of her thoughts were there, in the present with me.

We stopped and turned to look up at the walnut tree for a while, and Molly's grip on my arm kept getting tighter and tighter. Finally, she lowered her gaze to the ground for a few seconds, then looked up at me.

"Okay," she said. She turned to face me, pulled down on my arm, and stood up on her toes so she could kiss me, then she started pulling me away toward the fallen tree again.

We turned away from the clearing, but just then came a high-pitched chattering sound from the walnut tree. I looked up again, then nudged Molly.

Up amid the highest branches of the tree, just peeking over from the far side, sat a huge gray squirrel, the biggest squirrel I've ever seen—almost the size of a cat. It was clearly scolding us for some reason, looking down directly at us from its perch and screeching its grievances.

"Whoa," breathed Molly.

I took a step forward, and the squirrel grew even louder. I kept walking toward it, towing Molly with me, until I stood at the very edge of the clearing. It stuck to its opinion—whatever it was—and to its perch. Something in me wondered what would happen if I walked up to the tree and touched it. Would the squirrel flee then—leap away into the branches of one of the other trees outside the circle? Or would it—and I swear to you, this thought came into my mind—would it come down to the ground, to scold me to my face? Or even speak to me in my own language? How else was I supposed to understand?

I watched it for almost a minute, trying to make myself take the next step into the clearing, but I had never before set foot inside the circle of trees. Every time I had passed this way and looked up at the great walnut, something had held me back, and it was the same this time. I tried to tell myself to ignore the voice in the back of my mind warning me that some secrets were meant to stay in the forest. *The forest doesn't have secrets*, the rational part of my brain assured me. But I still couldn't take that step. Eventually, Molly gave my arm another squeeze, and I looked down at her.

"I love you," she said.

I smiled, and the uneasiness just fluttered away in an instant. "I love you," I said.

"Come on," said Molly, and she pulled me away from the clearing.

The fallen tree lay just twenty yards or so farther from the clearing. I held onto her arm so she could step over the trunk and sit down facing toward the west. She snuggled up to me as I sat down next to her, and we watched the sun set for a while, feeling each other's breath ebb and flow. The sky had already turned pink and orange across the horizon, and you could almost look directly at it through the screen of the tree branches. In another two weeks, it would be impossible to see the sunset from this place.

When the sun was just kissing the top edge of the horizon, Molly took a deep breath. "This is the last time I'll come out here," she said.

I said nothing. I knew she was right, even though I kept hoping we would have another chance.

After another few seconds, when I didn't say anything, she said, "I thought I was through all the stages of grief, you know? All the way into acceptance? I've been thinking about it, watching myself to make sure I give myself all the time I needed in each stage. But I don't think I'm really there. I really thought I was there when we went over all my bank accounts and social media accounts and everything else. It was like, 'You only do this if you know you're dying, so I must really know,' you know? But I'm still... god, I guess I'm just still afraid."

I dug my fingers into her side, then relaxed them—didn't want to hurt her. I could only nod. If I'd admitted I was afraid, too, I'd have fallen apart.

Molly sat up a little so she could turn and look at me. "It's not exactly about regrets, either," she said. "I mean, that's in there. I was going to do so much with my life, you know? We're still pretty young. That... that sucks. I really wanted to raise kids with you. But it's not just that."

She pressed herself against me again and looked out at the sinking sun. "Yeah, it's not just that," she said. "I'm actually really scared, honey. I'm scared." And she laughed this weak, self-conscious little laugh. "Some rational adult I am."

I cleared my throat to make sure I'd be able to speak clearly. "It's not irrational," I said. "It's natural to fear the unknown. You might even say it's rational."

"I'm not afraid of the unknown," said Molly. "I know what comes next: nothing."

I stiffened, but she persisted. "People talk about it like we just don't know which kind of nice-sounding afterlife is coming, but that's just wishful thinking. This is what we get, and it's almost over for me. I'm not afraid of dying, I'm afraid of not existing anymore." Her voice started to crack just a little. "I'll just... stop. Why should that be so terrifying? But it is. It really is."

She squeezed me as tightly as she could, and I swallowed again, trying to keep my throat from tightening up and getting raw. "I just... can't believe that," I said. "I can't believe everything just stops because I can't... there's no way there isn't more—more than what we can see right here in front of us. I can feel the more that there is—feel it in the sunset and the leaves and your warmth against my body. There's more to everything—more to us."

Molly sat up and pulled her arm away from my waist so she could reach up with both hands to bring my face down to hers. Her kiss—long and deep and full of the passion she always kept back for just these kinds of moments—drove away my fear for a brief instant, and when she pulled away from me again she was smiling through her tears.

"I know," she said. "I love that you believe in more. I love that—whatever that is in you that makes you so sure there's some Other thing, no matter how little sense that makes to me. You're so wrong, but I love it. I love you."

"I love you," I said, and I kissed her forehead so I could stop staring into her eyes before I burst into tears. "And I'm not wrong."

"Okay," said Molly, nestling back up against me. "As long as I can have you with me, telling yourself we'll see each other again, maybe I can be brave enough to leave you forever."

I said nothing. I couldn't speak, or I'd have come undone. So we sat together, watching the ground swallow up the sun, and the trees watched with us. When only the last edge of the sun lingered above the horizon, Molly cleared her throat.

"Will you sing to me?" she asked, and I thought I heard her voice break again, just a little. "One more song at sunset?"

I wanted to wander off into the woods alone and weep until my voice was gone. I didn't want to sing.

"What song should I sing?" I asked, stalling.

"The new one," said Molly. "Sing me something new, something that comes next."

I definitely did not want to sing the new song. It was stuck. I'd started with a fragment of John Donne's "Eclogue" that spoke to me, but I hadn't made any progress on adding words of my own—not since Molly's condition had been deemed terminal. She must have suspected I wouldn't finish it in time for her to hear it. And I couldn't refuse to sing it. I sat in silence for as long as I dared, trying to clear my mind so I wouldn't picture her face as I sang. After a while, when the sun had finally disappeared and left the sky darkening into blood orange and cobalt, I took a deep breath and sang out as strong as I could.

> *First her eyes kindle other ladies' eyes,*
> *Then from their beams their jewels' lustres rise,*
> *And from their jewels torches do take fire,*
> *And all is warmth, and light, and good desire.*
> *Most other courts, alas! are like to hell,*
> *Where in dark places, fire without light doth dwell;*

Or but like stoves; for lust and envy get
Continual, but artificial heat.
Here zeal and love grown one all clouds digest,
And make our court an everlasting east.

"*East*" echoed out into the fading light of the west as I
fell silent. After a few seconds Molly knew I wouldn't sing
any more, and she turned to look up at me again. I
couldn't avoid her gaze, so I looked down and saw tears
running down her face again.

"You still don't have anything else?"

I shook my head. If I'd said even a word, everything
would have come rushing out, and I couldn't—couldn't
break down and weep, or tell her that I never had time to
work; that I was worn out and stressed out already with
taking care of her; that even when I could find time to sit
down and pick at new words or new melodies, I felt like
that part of my brain had gone dead. I couldn't say any of
those things, even if I was sure that Molly already knew
them all. So I only shook my head, then looked up at the
sky again.

Molly kept looking up at me for almost a minute, but I
pretended to be enamored of the sunset. Finally, her whole
body relaxed, and she let go of me.

"We should go home before it gets dark," she said, in
this small, flat voice.

"Okay," I said.

She stood up, and I helped her back over the fallen
tree. She kept her eyes on the ground as we walked back
toward the path, but she let me hold her hand again.

As we passed by The Dryads' Circle—which is how I thought of the clearing around the walnut tree—I caught a flicker of green above our heads. I looked up at the great walnut, and I caught my breath.

It was on fire. The tops of its uppermost branches were burning—green-colored flames like translucent leaves of grass licking at the bark but not consuming it. I glanced at the trees around it, but they bore only the small, fragile leaves of early spring.

"What's wrong?" asked Molly, looking up at me as I slowed down to stare at the tree.

"Nothing," I said. "I… I thought I saw something."

"Oh," said Molly, returning her gaze to the ground.

I looked back at the tree for as long as I could while we walked away. The long shadows of sunset had faded into the twilight, but the green flames were casting faint shadows of their own. Eventually, when I couldn't see the walnut any longer, I looked down at my shape and Molly's as we trudged back to the main path.

Instead of growing fainter, I realized the shadows were growing darker, clearer, more defined. I looked up again, back over my shoulder, and the fire was spreading. Igniting treetop after treetop, it was catching up to us, setting the whole forest alight. As we merged back onto the path, the green flames reached it too, and then they started to spread in the direction of our house, lighting our way for us into the darkness.

3

This night, though, the fire faded out before I reached the edge of the forest. It didn't matter; I knew where I was. I had found the main path again, and I raced through the trees. Before long I could see the lights of the house shimmering in the distance. I ran past the barn and stopped running only when I reached the short wooden staircase leading up to the kitchen door.

I can't quite describe my sensations as I took off my dirty shoes and opened the door to go into the kitchen. My heart was pounding—and not just from the run. It was exhilarating, escaping from such danger and darkness and terror back into the safety and light, but now that I was standing under the soft yellow glow of the ceiling fan light on the green-tiled floor, I wondered if I was letting my imagination run away with me. Here on the threshold of death itself, was I giving in to fantasies I thought I'd left behind in childhood? That made more sense than believing that some kind of giant was roaming around in the woods, or that a fire spirit was protecting me. I'd gone out in a black mood, and I'd carried my despair and resentment with me into the forest. I shouldn't be surprised if a place I'd always half-believed to be magical reflected those feelings back to me in physical form—not when I was already in such a spiritually vulnerable state.

I tried to shake some sense back into my head, to come back to the present, and I realized I'd been standing with my shoes in my hand for over a minute. I dropped them on the mat by the door and crossed at once through the hallway into the living room.

Molly was sitting up on the couch, looking up the hallway as I entered the living room, as though she'd been staring that direction for hours, waiting for me.

My heart jumped up into my throat again, and I ran the rest of the way to the couch. "Oh my god, Molly!" I said. "I'm sorry, honey! How long have you been awake? Are you okay?"

The corners of her mouth twitched as I reached her—the most of her smile that I usually got to see now. I kissed her cheek, and she made a vague kissing motion with her lips in the air next to my face. As I was turning to fetch the blood pressure cuff and thermometer from the credenza where we kept them, I heard the click in her throat that meant she was trying to speak. I turned the TV down so I could hear her—not that we kept it very loud; it was just on to give her something to look at. It took her a few tries, but she managed to at least start the words as I was slipping the cuff onto her arm.

"Fine…" she said. "Not long."

"Oh, good," I said, as I pumped the cuff tight. "I'm sorry I wasn't here when you woke up. I love you so much, you know that, right?"

Molly nodded, then started trying to form words again. "Don't…" she said, and I think she was trying to nod toward the blood-pressure cuff. "Fine. I'm… fine. Go back to work."

"Just checking your vitals. I haven't done it today," I said.

"Doesn't matter," she said. "Not… now."

"No, don't say that," I said. "We need to keep you as healthy as we can."

I clocked her pulse as I released the pressure in the cuff. "Pretty good," I said as I slipped it off her arm. "One-twenty-seven over eighty-three. Quitting the blood-pressure meds was a good call."

Molly gave a jerky little nod, then slumped back against the couch. She followed me with her eyes as I put the blood pressure cuff back and brought the thermometer over to her temple.

"Temperature's good, too," I said. "No fever today."

Molly lifted her head a little again. When I turned around from putting back the thermometer, she had raised her arm, and she was waving me away.

"Go, work," she whispered.

"No, I'm done for the day," I said. "Do you need anything? Are you cold?"

She rolled her head back and forth on the couch. "No, work," she said again. Her eyes were getting wider. She was pleading with me, begging me to be normal.

"Are you thirsty? Hungry?" Molly rolled her head again, still staring at me with her giant, insistent eyes.

"I really am done for the day," I lied. "Are you sure you don't need anything?"

Molly struggled, trying to sit up. I helped her, and she did her best to glare at me.

"I know… you're lying," she said. "Just… sit with me, if… if you're not going to work."

The last few words came tumbling out together in one breath, and she slumped back onto the couch. I looked down at her, and I couldn't decide which hurt more—that she knew, and it made her sad, or that she had lost the strength or will to berate me. Finally, I just turned and sat down next to her. I took her hand and held it, and we sat watching one of her many sci-fi dramas until she fell asleep again an hour or so later.

The next day, Molly was asleep again when I woke up. I lay on my little trestle bed at the other end of the living room, watching her breathing for a while, but I couldn't do it for long. I got up, I showered, and when I checked on her again she was still asleep. I put the little device that would call my phone on the arm of the couch, where she would be able to reach it when she woke up, and I went to my studio.

Molly built my studio for me first thing when we moved in. She did it all herself: read all these articles and watched videos about soundproofing, and clean power, and built this amazing audio workstation for me, even though I told her I'd mostly just use the piano and some staff paper.

"What you do is so incredible," she'd said. "You should have all the best tools. I know you won't use the recording gear much, but when you do—you don't want to have to make a bunch of trips into the city to record. You get so much done when you can live in your own world."

And she'd been right. That first album I recorded there—*Molotov*—went so much smoother—like I was just singing it into existence, like the audio interfaces and the software didn't even exist. The songs just all of a sudden existed in digital form, straight out of my brain. I'd had to lock myself in that studio for weeks at a time to accomplish it, but they felt like hours to me, even if they didn't to Molly. It really did become my world, my cocoon, my incubator.

Now, every time I went into that studio, it felt like a prison.

I closed the door behind me, then checked my phone for the fourth time in a row to make sure the app that would respond to the call button was really running. Then I set it on the piano, off to one side just a little. Shuffled my notes and my blank staff paper. Moved my pencil to just the right place above the keys. Played a few scales. Then I sat with my hands in my lap for three minutes, just staring at the blank pages, willing myself to sing.

"Fine, just anything," I muttered to myself at last, and I started playing "Martha My Dear" by the Beatles, just to warm up. Then it was "Trouble" from Over the Rhine's *The Trumpet Child*. Then "Extraordinary Machine" by Fiona Apple.

"Oh my god, what is wrong with you," I said to myself, thumping my fists down onto the keys as I reached the middle of the second line.

I put my hands in my lap again, then put them back on the keys again almost right away. Then I said to myself, "Here," and I started to play the opening bars of one of my earliest songs, a popular one I'd played live so many times I could do it without thinking.

I'm not up here to make you like me.
Your pats and praises don't excite me.
Every spark that's not my own will gutter before it ignites me,
And I get to choose what defines me,
Inspires me,
Has the power to flatter or spite me;
I'll write me.
I'll write me.
I'll write me.

But that's not really true anymore, is it? I thought, as I pounded the keys. (The piano really takes a beating for "Write Me.") *Someone got in; someone ignites me. Or did.*

"You were so enchanting," Molly had said about the first time she saw me perform live. We hadn't met yet, but I remember her, too—sitting a few rows back in this old, half-derelict church auditorium in Northern Indiana, staring up at me with those giant eyes and that giant smile, with her hands balled up under her chin, so enraptured that she barely moved for two hours. As soon as my eyes landed on her I knew I had her under my spell for the night.

The spell had worn off, I guess. More powerful, darker magic had defeated my own. I couldn't work any magic powerful enough, now, not even to bewitch her mind for a few minutes at a time, to pull her back up out of the half-life she was living in these last few days, just for a little while. I couldn't even finish one song, with this darkness seeping into my mind. And what was the point of finishing it? Was I going to jump back three months and sing it to her when she asked for it, at the time when she most needed me to alter reality for her—make her believe, just for a moment, that she could cling to me and my song, that we could anchor her soul to this world? Even if I could have waved my hands—danced them along the keys and conjured up the old enchantments —their potency had evaporated.

I smashed my hands down onto the keys as "Write Me" came to a close, and I just sat there, my nose inches above the keyboard.

"Nnngghhhh," I growled through my teeth, with my eyes clenched shut, digging my fingernails into my palms. "Come on!"

The keys squalled at me as I pushed myself back up, away from the keyboard. I shuffled a single piece of staff paper to the center and stuck my pencil behind my ear, and I started in on the Eclogue.

First her eyes kindle other ladies' eyes,
Then from their beams their jewels' lustres rise,
And from their jewels torches do take fire,
And all is warmth, and light, and good desire.
Most other courts, alas! are like to hell,

Where in dark places, fire without light doth dwell;
Or but like stoves; for lust and envy get
Continual, but artificial heat.
Here zeal and love grown one all clouds digest,
And make our court an everlasting east.

Concentrating on the words was good. *Yes, yes, here it is*, I was thinking, as I let my hands move into a new progression when the familiar chords came to an end. They petered out after a bar or two—just dissolved into the ether, where I couldn't quite retrieve them. But they had been there. I had heard them, and played them. I could conjure them again. I backed up two lines and started over.

Here zeal and love grown one all clouds digest,
And make our court an everlasting east.

And then the new chords again, just for a measure or two before I found my fingers skidding around at a loss. I took out my pencil and scrawled a few notes on the paper, gaps in the places where my memory misfired. Then I dropped it back on the rack and started again, farther back this time.

Most other courts, alas! are like to hell,
Where in dark places, fire without light doth dwell;
Or but like stoves; for lust and envy get
Continual, but artificial heat.

Before I could get to the end this time, and try to loosen up just a little more to let my instincts take over, my eyes caught a flicker of unexpected color at the door. I wouldn't have seen it except that I was actually getting into the song, you know? Actually giving in, letting my head move with my hands, and that was how I came to even see her, standing still with a blank expression just out of my eyeline—if I had been keeping my eyes on the keys.

4

I swiveled away from the piano, trying to keep the frustration out of my face. "What is it, honey?"

"I...." Molly dragged in a long, slow breath. Her eyes shifted around a bit before finding mine. Even then they were pleading with me to understand. Then I saw that she was holding her pillow to her chest with one hand. Farther down, her sweatpants had turned dark around the crotch.

"Did you wet the couch again?" I said.

Molly nodded: a long, slow nod, once up and once down. I inhaled a long breath of my own.

"Okay," I said, and I put on my cheerful tone so she wouldn't think she was being a burden. I got up and walked across to take the pillow from her. "That's okay, honey. That's okay. Let's just get you into the shower."

Molly nodded again and gave me another one of her tiny smiles, and I said, "Come on, here we go. It's okay."

I took her arm and helped her turn around, out toward the stairs.

She was still too heavy for me to carry by myself, so going upstairs took several minutes, one step at a time. I peeled off her clothes in the bathroom and helped her into the shower, onto her stool, and made sure she could reach everything before I took her clothes downstairs. I just balled them up and tossed them on the floor at the head of the basement stairs. First I had to clean up the couch.

We had put a protective vinyl cover over it when she started to lose bladder control, so cleanup wasn't that hard anymore. I filled up a bucket with bleach water and took the rag to it, but there wasn't much to clean up; Molly only drank a few mouthfuls of water a day by then.

I poured the bucket down the sink in the mudroom and rinsed it out. Then I thought about checking on Molly, but I knew she wouldn't be done showering yet. She liked to just sit under the warm water, and she wouldn't need my help for a while, so I... I just went back to my studio. I walked over to the piano and looked down at the keys—just standing there, with my arms by my sides.

The few brief chords I had scratched onto the staff paper still sat there, but they made no sense to me now. Even humming them over in my head, I could tell they were wrong. Wrong. Like I was working on a totally different song, for someone else to sing. Someone who would be disappointed, probably. Well, I wouldn't get anything else written that day. Molly would need help washing her hair, then getting dressed, then getting back down to the couch, and then I would need to make us lunch, and try to get her to eat, then clean up after lunch, then try to get her interested in something, then give up and just sit beside her while she stared at the TV without seeing a single thing that happened on the screen, until I had to fight the urge to check her pulse every three minutes to make sure she hadn't gone.

No more composing today. I would just have to sit and pound out my brains against the keyboard tomorrow.

I stared at those hateful chords: just a few little pencil marks that somehow told me I would never be able to finish another song again, that everything that made me special and powerful and—and *me*—it was all atrophying and getting dragged down into the earth, along with Molly. I stood there, and I didn't realize it, but my chest was starting to heave, and my teeth were clenched, and after a few seconds I just raised my hand and swept everything off the piano, across the room. The papers went flying, and my pencil clattered against the far wall, and I stood watching it all, shaking—just shaking, my hands balled up into fists. I so furiously wanted to cry right then, without Molly there to see me, but something else had ahold of me, and so I just stood there, breathing through my teeth.

Then, upstairs, I heard a thump, and I went flying out of the room and up the stairs. I banged through the bathroom door and wrenched back the shower curtain, and there was Molly, just sitting, staring at the bottle of shampoo that was rolling around on the floor—where she had dropped it.

"Here you go, honey," I said, and I reached into the water and picked up the shampoo bottle. "I can do it."

I washed her hair, then helped her dry off, and we went back downstairs.

Molly actually seemed more awake when we got back to the couch, so I pulled over the card table that had her half-finished model of Howl's Moving Castle. She had been feeling optimistic a few weeks before, and started a new project that I knew now she was never going finish. The little Lego blocks still lay around the legs of the castle where she had staged them, but she hadn't shown any real interest in it for a while. I would put it within reach, and she would pick up the bricks and look at them, or hold one of them up to the model, but she just couldn't hold complex spatial concepts like that in her mind anymore. She always ended up just staring at the model, then falling asleep in an awkward position with her head still resting on the arm of the couch and her arms stretched out across it toward the model. This time, I swore to myself I'd move it away if she started looking lost and full of despair again, before it had a chance to drag her down.

She started at once trying to fit one of the blocks into place, and she was almost getting it right. I went into the kitchen and started fixing our lunch: a sandwich for me, and a small bowl of yogurt for her: as much as I thought she could manage, which wasn't much. I was just putting the spoon into the bowl and getting ready to carry it out to her, and feeling pretty good about myself because I had just looked into the living room and Molly was still working on the model, when someone knocked on the door.

I set down the bowl and went to answer it. There, waiting on the big wraparound front porch, was someone I'd never expected to see again in any lifetime: Molly's old high-school friend Annie. They hadn't spoken in years— since the night before our wedding, in fact—and it could have been longer for all I cared.

She'd been looking out toward the road when I opened the door, and she spun around like a startled deer. Her eyes were huge, like she'd just been slapped in the face and hadn't realized she should be angry yet. I saw her swallow, and she licked her lips twice before she could even get any words out, but I wanted to have the first word, anyway.

"What makes you think you can show up here?" I said.

And before she can even answer, I step out onto the porch with her and shut the door behind me. The sky beyond the porch had turned slate-gray since the night before, and the air had that stuffy, tense feel that could only mean a storm. Right now, that gathering storm was me.

"I…" Annie says. And she swallows again. "I know you don't want to see me," she says. "I'm… I'm sorry. I didn't know about… about… Molly. I just found out. I would've come before, but I didn't know. I'm sorry. I know—does she… would she see me? I know I hurt her pretty bad."

"Yeah," I say, not softening it at all. "Yeah, you hurt her really, really badly."

Her eyes widen even more. Didn't expect that from the quiet person who'd let herself be insulted all those years ago. I'd kept my mouth shut then; she was Cara's friend, not mine. But she'd always looked scared, I think. People-pleaser. Can't say what's on her mind until it's too late, and it's going to explode, and she does something she regrets. Like this.

"I know; I'm sorry!" she wails. "I know… I know it hurt you, too. I hated myself for so long, I really did. I never meant to—"

I cut in. "To what? To try to come between me and the person I love? To make Molly feel worthless and abandoned? Well, you fucked up, because that's what you did. You weren't there to see it, but she was brave at the wedding. So brave. She was the warrior inside that I've always known she was—"

Annie nods her agreement with this, anxious to get back on the right footing, but I'm not having her trying to get herself somehow on the same side as me.

"Yeah, you should have known what you had in her. The best friend a person could hope for, wasn't she? And she really cared about you. She was miserable about you, and if she hadn't had me… well, if she hadn't had me, she'd have had you, wouldn't she?"

"I'm sorry," she says again. Her voice is barely above a whisper now, and she makes this empty, hand-clutching gesture in the air, like she wants to take hold of me but doesn't dare. "I hated myself so much, and… and I wanted to apologize, but I was—I'm so stubborn and proud, sometimes. If I hadn't heard she was sick, I might never have—"

"No, you don't get to have her just so you can feel good about yourself again," I say. "You don't get show up in her last…." Something clogs my throat, and I have to take a deep breath, and swallow, before I can go on. And my voice gets quieter then—more even, but more intense.

"You don't get to show up in Molly's last days on earth, and salve your conscience—try to rewrite the book on what kind of person you've been. No. No, that's not happening."

"That's not what—"

"Oh, it's not? Tell me what it's about, then—go on."

"I do understand," she says, and her voice is cracking, tears in her eyes now. "I understand: I was wrong. I should have accepted you. I should have accepted that you were Molly's choice; you were who she loved. I want to tell her that, please. And you—I want you to know. I should have put aside my own personal belief about it, and I should have—"

I can feel my face getting hot, and adrenaline pounding in my throat, but I don't care, and I don't wait for her to finish.

"You know, I had weeks and months and years to think about it, and I don't even believe you," I say. "I don't believe it was really me you objected to. I was just a convenient excuse: an excuse to do what some part of you wished you could do for a long time before that. Molly got out of your snot-nosed little bigoted town, but you had to stay, didn't you? You had to stay and be conventional, and —*small*. Molly went out and lived, and all that business about her 'turning into a different person'—that wasn't about me. That was about her and you."

Annie's shrinking away from me now, tears running down her face, and she's shaking her head, but I'm relentless, and I'm getting louder, and I feel like I'm getting bigger—towering over her and backing her off the porch, back out of our lives again.

"And now—now when she's sick and vulnerable, and you get to feel strong and whole when you look at her— *now* is when you show up with your apology and your repentance? No. Those are for you. I don't know what Molly could get from seeing you right now, except more pain," I say. "I know what you get out of it. You get to relieve your conscience... such as it is. Well, go see your fucking pastor for that."

She's wilted now, not even able to look me in the eye, but she's stopped crying. She wipes her face with the back of her hand, then straightens up, and then she does look at me.

"You're wrong," she says. "My world was only smaller because Molly wasn't in it anymore. It's fine if you don't believe me, but she should have a chance to decide for herself."

My breath is still coming sharp and short, and I'm in no mood to admit she has a point, so I just glare at her.

She says, "I... I know she doesn't have much longer." And the tears start to form in her eyes again. "I'm staying in town, at the Red Roof. I'll be there, until... for as long as she's here, I'll be here. Please tell her... please?"

I just stare at her. The fire is dying down in my chest and my temples, and I notice again how raw my throat feels. I can't refuse a request like that, phrased like that. But I can't say yes, either. So there we stand, until finally she wipes her eyes again and turns away without another word. I watch her until she gets in her rental car and drives away, kicking up dust all down the drive. Then my hand finds the doorknob, and I go back inside.

I pass the living room on the way back to the kitchen, and I see Molly—not reaching out for her model anymore, but staring toward the front door, toward me. And even with her eyes half-drained of expression, like they always were then, her reproach cuts right through my soul. She heard. She heard everything.

5

After an eternity, I tear my eyes from hers, but I can feel her gaze on me as I stomp back to the kitchen. To avoid seeing that look again—disappointed and hurt and… lonely, somehow—I grab her clothes that I balled up at the basement door earlier and forgot about. I wrench open the basement door and start down the stairs, but I only get a few steps down before something cuts through my anger and defensiveness, and self-righteousness.

The steps… feel wrong. They're made of old wood, but it's always been solid, if a little creaky, especially in the dead of night. Now it feels soft under my feet—squishy and organic and uneven. I look down at my feet. In the light coming in through the kitchen windows above, I can see vines, twining themselves around the steps and the sides of the staircase. They haven't gotten up to the last few stairs—I look behind me to check—but the bottom stairs are thick with them. Halfway up, where I'm standing, several coils loop around each step. They're even starting to crawl their way up the walls on either side of the staircase: thinner tendrils of curling green—a sick, shiny green that makes me recoil as soon as I notice it.

I start to walk down, one careful step at a time, and that's when I realize the basement is just not the same place I remember. The hard, dry, packed dirt floor has turned soggy, even wet in places. Even from where I'm standing—and I can only see about a ten-foot radius from the middle of the staircase—there are a few puddles, and one of them has algae growing on it. As I take another step, then another, and I get to where I can duck my head below the level of the ceiling, my heart almost stops beating.

There are no walls. I think… I almost think I can see them at first, but the darkness in the basement has come alive. There are vines hanging down from the ceiling, and they glow a little in the darkness: iridescent green that puts a kink in my stomach. Beyond each hanging vine—again, I almost think I can see the wall at the far end of the basement, which should be just twenty or twenty-five feet away—around each vine the air seems to twist, like two realities are fighting to present themselves. I wished I had turned on the light as I came down from the head of the stairs, but I so rarely need it. I know my way… or I'd thought I did.

I'm still clutching Molly's clothes in my hand, and there—so strange to see it sitting near the bottom of the steps, surrounded by vines and puddles of murky water—there's the washing machine, ready for me to toss them in. I take another step, but I just can't bring myself to go any farther—to set foot on that swampy floor. Who knows what would happen? I close my eyes and take a long, slow, deep breath, all the way down into my diaphragm, but when I open my eyes nothing has changed. I tighten my grip on the stair rail. Maybe it was my imagination, but far off in the distance, I hear a faint *plop*, and I feel something start to crawl over my little finger on the railing.

I jump back, then just chuck the ball of clothes onto the washer. I didn't stay to watch them land—just ran back up the stairs two at a time. I slam the door behind me and lean against it, trying to tell myself that nothing is coming up behind me, that there's no reason to be holding the door shut like this. The kitchen looks normal enough: full of warm afternoon light. I straighten up and take a step or two away from the basement door, but I don't dare turn and look at it until after I've washed my hands. Even then I only spare it a glance as I carry the bowl of yogurt out to Molly in the living room.

Molly didn't have anything to say about my outburst just then, and she fell asleep again not long after eating her three spoonfuls of yogurt. I sat beside her with my arm stretched out across the back of the couch and stroked her forehead whenever she stirred in her sleep, and just watched TV while the room went dark then light again as the sun started to set. The living room faces west, and the sun casts long shadows over everything as it goes down, and it shows up all the dust floating in the air because neither of us ever clean anything.

The storm hadn't broken yet, and the sky was still overcast, so the shadows weren't so stark. And it was a good thing, because if I'd had to watch that dark line creep across the floor toward me as the sun disappeared, like the night itself invading my house and overtaking me, I might have run again. Instead, everything just got grayer and grayer, until the TV started to hurt my eyes. I was just about to get up and turn on the lights when Molly stirred and opened her eyes. She curled her head around and looked at me, then smiled that same little half-smile.

"Hi," I said.

"Hi," said Molly.

"Do you need anything?"

She turns her head slowly to one side, then the other. "Just you."

I smile. "I'm here."

Her smile fades a little, and she wiggles the fingers of one hand a little, curling the tips toward herself. I put my hand in hers, and she gives it a tiny squeeze.

"That's...." Her breath fails her, and she tries to take a nice, slow, cautious breath. "That's... all you have... have to do," she says. "Just... be here."

"Okay," I say.

"Just be you," says Molly. "That's... all now. Don't need a... don't need you to f... fight for me... or prot... tect me."

"But I will," I say. "I always will. Just try to stop me." And I give her kind of a wicked grin. But she won't have it.

"That... that wasn't you," she says. "Out there." And she gives her head a little jerk upward, gesturing over her shoulder, toward the front door.

I stiffen. If I could have pulled my hand away from hers, I would have. But it was hers. She could have it forever.

"You're… you've gone somewhere," Molly says. "I know you… can't write."

"It's just a phase," I say. "I'll get there."

She gives her head a little shake again. "It's… eating you," she says. "I'm taking you down… with me. I know. I know, because… cuz that… out there… wasn't you. Wasn't you."

"I'm sorry," I say, trying to mean it as much as I can. "I shouldn't have said all those things to her. But she—"

I cut my excuse short as Molly closes her eyes. I know that look. She doesn't want to hear any more. After a few seconds she looks at me again.

"Just be," she says, and her eyes get a little wider, her tone of voice a little more expressive than it has been the last few days. Earnestness—or urgency—that's what it was.

"I know… 's almost… over. All I… need is you. Just… be… and I'll know… 's a promise… or, not that. A guarantee? Got… to know you'll… keep it alive… us alive. Be… the mmm… 'mazing person I love. Help me… help me go… guarantee. Hope… go with hope. Hope what… w's best of us… outlive… me."

She closed her eyes after that speech, but I could tell she wasn't asleep. My throat ached, but I tried to swallow it away. I couldn't start crying, not when she had just told me how much she needed me. But if I tried to tell her how lost I felt, or that I had no idea how to be the person she wanted me to be when she was fading out of my world, I would have fallen to pieces at that moment. Instead, I just cleared my throat, and tried to say the words she wanted to hear.

"I know it will," I said. "I know you'll always be with me. What's best of you… what makes you *you* will live on. I'll keep you alive in my heart."

I hated myself the second the words left my mouth.

Molly's lips tensed. She opened her eyes and looked at me, then took a deep breath and let it out.

"Sure," she breathed, in her same flat tone—done listening to me lie.

Then she started trying to sit up, so I reached over and pulled her up by her arms. But what she really wanted was to curl up and put her head in my lap. She folded her arms close to her chest, and I started stroking her hair.

I knew I had to do better. That couldn't be the end of the conversation. I couldn't let her last days—or hours—be full of lies, me shielding her from my worst fears and ugliest thoughts just to give her some kind of false cheerfulness in the face of death. She knew. She would always know. And that was worse to her than whatever terrible truth I might feel like I needed to hide.

So after a long time sitting and going over all this in my mind, I finally steel myself, and I start talking, even though I don't know what's going to come out.

"I—I'm trying," I say. "I know you just want me to keep doing what I always do. I want—I wish I could keep making things you love, but it's… it's so hard right now, Molly. It's so much… I don't know how to fulfill all this… promise. Your life… being cut short—it can't all be on me to make it count, to live enough and—and accomplish enough, for both of us. You made this place for us—for me, really. But it's a… soon it's just going to be full of ghosts. It's not going to be a home anymore, not a safe place for me to live the kind of life you want me to have… to live for you. I… I'm sorry, honey. This makes me sound so… I'm so pathetic, I'm sorry. Complaining about how hard this is for me, but really you're…."

Then I realize: she's asleep again. Somewhere in the middle of my long, self-indulgent rambling, she'd drifted away again, to the edges of wherever she was lingering in those last few days. So I just kept running my fingers over her hair, looking down at her face, so much more relaxed and like herself in sleep.

The sun had gone down by that time, I think. I could still see a faint glow against the clouds, but most of the sky had blackened in the twilight. The TV was still on, now casting its own shadows throughout the room, which darkened or faded as the screen flickered. The air felt thick, even inside the house, like the storm gathering outside had somehow wormed its tendrils in under the windows—or maybe something else had.

A deep, low rumble came up from the ground: the first of the thunder. I could almost feel it in my bones, that the rain was coming, and it came with the second roll of thunder, the first few droplets tapping on the rooftop. Then the tapping grew into a rhythm, and the rhythm into a roar, and before long, the rain was lashing at the windows, and the thunder was rattling the glass. The wind swept all around the house, changing its direction every few seconds, it seemed, and battering us from the outside, me and Molly. The whole sky had gone black, and the lightning only made the darkness greater. It split the skies over and over, with the thunder only half a second behind now, and every time the purple glow faded out, the blackness closed in tighter, and heavier.

I only sat still on the couch, my fingers tangled in Molly's hair, holding my breath every time the lightning struck—holding it until the darkness rolled back over us. Something told me this rain would never wash away my fears, or my despair, but maybe the darkness would swallow me up and make me as if I had never been. Maybe the lightning would burn me up to nothing, or the wind batter something out of me: whatever had me seized up inside, unable to find relief.

Then, without quite knowing how, or how long I had been watching the sky change, unseeing, I realized that the darkness outside was not so dark. A light was growing—flickering, and sometimes dwindling again by degrees, but definitely growing brighter, just outside the west-facing window.

I glanced over my shoulder at the eastern side of the house, but there, the blackness was still black. When I turned west again, the difference almost took my breath away. The light outside had overpowered the television, casting a green tinge over the entire room. I looked down at Molly's face, pale green and smoothed by the even cast of light from the window. She was still sleeping, and not likely to wake even for an earth-shaking storm like this. I raised her up a little off my lap and levered myself out from under her head, then pulled a cushion over to take my place. Then I crept over to the window, almost as though I expected to find something—or someone—waiting outside, watching for me. When I saw the source of the light, I actually gasped, and I pressed myself up against the window, with my hands white-knuckling the window frame.

6

The barn was on fire. It was an old structure, empty since we moved in, and probably even before, and its wood had long ago begun to crumble and rot. And now it was burning, green fire blazing up from within it and curling up around the roof: the same green fire I'd seen last night, and two months before.

And just like before, the fire was not burning it up. The flames almost hid it from view, but the barn was still standing. I watched for—I don't even know for how long—but the fire kept burning, and the barn kept standing. Every now and then, I would see it shake when a really strong blast of wind hit it, and each time I would be sure that this was the beginning of when it would crumble and finally burn up. But if anything, it was the wind that was doing more to tear it apart. The barn began to shake more and more with every new assault against it. I was holding my breath again, and digging my fingers into the wood of the window frame, and when the first board tore away from the barn and went tumbling across the field I let out a cry. I looked back at Molly, but she was still sleeping. I took a deep breath, trying to get calm, then I looked out the window again.

More boards were starting to peel off the barn, and the fire inside it was dying down. Somehow, though, I felt—I knew—knew with the deepest part of my soul—that it wasn't the wind or the rain that was quenching the fire. It was something else. Something from outside, from the darkness, was crushing in upon the source of the fire, and it was winning.

And it was crushing in upon me: I could feel it. The same dread—the same terror of the darkness—that I had felt in my bones the night before, out in the woods, was creeping over me again. I watched, frozen and silent at the window, as the lightning struck again and again, and with each flash and each crack of thunder, the darkness engulfed yet more and more of the green fire, until it—and I—seemed about to be swept away into nothingness at last.

Then the barn began to shake—shake from its foundation—and all at once the fire went out, leaving an even greater darkness. More and more boards went flying away, and the walls of the barn buckled. The whole thing shuddered—just convulsed, like something had seized hold of it—and I couldn't watch any more. I went flying back to the couch, to Molly. I threw myself to the floor next to her and buried my face in the cushions next to her legs. Outside, I could hear the barn cracking and groaning as it was torn to pieces.

I woke up the next morning on the floor next to the couch. I couldn't remember falling asleep, and I felt stiff and sore all over, in a way that just falling asleep on a hardwood floor couldn't entirely explain. The sun had come out after the storm, and the whole room was warm and yellow with its light. I picked myself up, groaning and wincing every time I hit a painful angle. Molly was still asleep, exactly as I had left her the night before, except that one of her fists was clutched against the side of her head. I kissed her forehead, but she kept still.

Looking around the room, trying to remember what I should do next to get ready for the day, my eyes fell on the window. I went over and looked out, and my heart began to pound in my chest when I saw exactly what I had known I would see—but hoped I wouldn't.

The barn was in pieces, strewn all across the field, and right up to the walls of the house—random boards and framing studs, some torn in half as the wind peeled them away from the structure. Where the barn floor used to be, a pile of the wreckage huddled on the ground, at the far end from the house. Some freak twist of the storm had left it in place, like a sort of cairn—a monument to what used to stand there. I felt this unaccountable curiosity to go out and look at it more closely. Now that the storm was over, and the sun was shining, the dread of the darkness and the fear I had felt when I saw the fire beaten down had fled away, and I wanted to see for myself what the storm had left behind.

I made sure Molly still had the little gadget that could summon me back to her, and I kissed her again on the temple. She looked cold, somehow, so I pulled a blanket over her, then kissed her again. Then I went out to the kitchen and pulled on the big rubber boots we kept for going outside in the mud after a rainstorm, and thumped down the wooden stairs to the ground.

No sooner had I started picking my way across the lawn, stepping over the occasional board and doing my best to avoid the worst of the mud patches, than I noticed something that should have come as more—or maybe less —of a surprise: none of the wood had been burned. Torn to bits, yes; blown and scattered into chaos, yes; but not burned. Not a single one of them bore any signs of even charring or scorching. Whatever had been burning inside the barn that night, it was no ordinary fire.

I had almost reached the small pile of rubble on the packed dirt surface of the barn floor when I heard a scraping and clicking noise away to my left. I looked, and there, coming up out of the storm door that led down into our basement, was a squirrel—a huge one. It had to be the same squirrel Molly and I had seen in the forest weeks ago; there couldn't be two squirrels that big.

The squirrel was watching me, staring right into my eyes as it twitched and jittered its way out of the ground. As I looked at it, it began chattering at me, just as it had done the first time.

"You're on my turf, now," I said to it. "And how'd you get into my basement?"

It just kept chattering, and I stared at it for a while before realizing—and this is really how I formed the thought in my head—that it had no intention of answering me. I turned back toward the pile of boards and kept walking.

The closer I got, the more the pile looked as though it had been built, not formed by accident—hastily thrown together, maybe, but built deliberately. The boards formed a rough triangle shape, rising up in criss-crossing layers to about the level of my knees. Or, at least, it had been that shape at first, but it looked as though someone or something had smashed into it from one side. And that made me second-guess myself. Maybe it only *looked* built from a certain angle. Maybe I was keyed up and feeling prickly and superstitious, ready to imbue anything with meaning whether it deserved it or not.

With only a few feet to go, a tiny shiver ran over my skin. At almost the exact same time, a few of the boards at the top of the pile shifted, and one of them slid off onto the ground. I froze, my heart in my mouth, and I stood that way, holding my breath, for almost ten seconds. But I didn't feel afraid. Not afraid, but curious—elated, almost. Something was under those boards, hiding, or protecting itself, from whatever had pursued it to this place, and I was about to find out what—and why.

I took another two steps forward and stood, looking down into the center of the pile, into the space at its heart. Between two of the planks that lay across the top of the little shelter, half-hidden in shadow, I saw a movement, and another shudder went through the pile—and through me. Then my eyes adjusted to the shadows, and I saw what I had come to see.

It was a woman—or a woman-shaped form, at least. Her skin was smooth and gray, or gray-green, like the bark of a tree, and she was slender, slender as a sickle moon, and naked. She had this wild tangle of hair, long and straight but standing almost directly out from her head, and it made her body look even thinner and smaller than it was. Her legs—too long for a human woman—were curled up against her chest, but her face was turned toward me. I could see her eyes, glinting green in the shadows, even though no direct light was shining in for them to reflect.

We looked at each other for a long time, she and I. Her face gave nothing away, and her eyes shone steadily, boring into mine. But gradually her body began to relax, and one of her hands that had been clutching her legs to her chest loosened its grip. I leaned forward and lifted up the boards that covered the top of her shelter, and she remained still and quiet as I tossed them aside. Then I stretched out my hand to her.

She reached up and took it in one of her own hands, long-fingered and hard, with sharp, pointed fingernails and thick knuckles—or, at least, they looked too thick for her thin fingers. Her skin felt smooth against mine, but hard, and her grip felt as though it could crush me. I pulled her to her feet, and she stood up straight and tall, even taller than me, and looked down at me with my hand still held in hers.

Looking at her unfolded, she was even more fantastical, like a woman who has been stretched up toward the sky by some unseen power. I took a step back from her, and she let go of my hand. We stood apart, and I could hear my own heartbeat—and I felt that she must be able to hear it, too. She looked as though she could see and hear and feel everything about me; I had no secrets from her, even after such a short time in her presence. Strangely, this thought gave me comfort, and courage, and I gathered myself to speak to her.

"Wh-who are you?" I asked, and my voice was hoarse and weak in my own ears.

She spoke, and her voice rasped at the edges, like the rattling of tree branches in the winter wind. "I am Karya," she said.

And my heart started beating even faster at the sound of her name. I felt that same sense of elation rush through me, so I took courage and made to speak again.

"Karya, how did you—"

But she cut across me, as though I had not spoken. "You must retrieve the fire," she said. "You must help me."

"I—what?" I said. "What do y—"

"You are at greatest risk," said Karya. "You will suffer most from its loss, and you must accept your blame."

"You—someone else," I said, and I was stumbling over my words. I could feel adrenaline starting to pound through my head. "You must mean someone else," I said. "I don't know what you mean. I—"

Then she leaned toward me—raised her long, reed-thin leg and stepped out of the pile of broken boards—and she gripped me by both arms. I could feel those long fingernails pressing into my flesh, but the pain was farthest from my mind. It was her eyes, piercing into mine. They cut through my doubt and injected me with certainty, even before she spoke again.

"I know you inside and out," she said. "I know you from ground to sky. What burned in me was ignited in you, and what has been quenched in you was taken from me. You are the only one who is able. You must retrieve the fire."

I looked up into her face, so unreadable except for those glowing eyes, which told me everything—everything—even though I couldn't put any of it into words. Part of me cried out that what she was saying made no sense, that none of this made sense, that such a being could not exist. But more of me—or the stronger part of me—knew she spoke the truth, even if I didn't understand it.

Then a new flutter of panic swept over me, and I remembered Molly, still sleeping back in the house. I twisted around to look in through the window: not that I could have seen her from where we stood, but I was seized with this sudden guilt and fear, that she would wake and find me gone—or, worse, make her way to the window and see me—doing what? What would she see?

"Do not be afraid," came the voice of the being that held me in its grip. "She will still be sleeping when you return."

My head spun back, and I looked into her eyes again. She knew. She knew my fear; she had understood the cry of my heart, had read my pain and guilt and found their source.

"Retrieve the fire," she said, "and I may be able to retrieve something of what you have lost as well. An exchange. But what you give will be worth more to you than what you receive."

I swallowed, and felt again how roughly my blood was pulsing in my throat. The fear had returned: the simple fear of the unknown, of this creature who held me in an unshakeable grip and fixed me with her strange, green-pupiled eyes, and of what she might require of me. But I didn't dare refuse. Not for fear of her, but because of that certainty. Because I knew that she was speaking the truth to me, whatever it was. She was speaking it to my soul, to my bones, to the core of me, and I would be a fool to refuse.

I swallowed again, and then I nodded, quickly, before I could regret it.

"Yes," said Karya. "You will know."

Then she pulled me toward her, both my arms still held in her unbreakable grasp. She pulled me close, leaning over me, until I could almost taste the earthy, organic smell of her. Then she pressed her lips to mine.

They were soft, softer than I would have thought, and warm. Their warmth spread through my whole body, then sent a shock of heat down through my very center. I felt as though I were burning from within, ready to burst into flames if she did not release me. Then I felt myself plummeting downward—not falling, but being dragged down, down into the earth. The ground opened up and swallowed me, and I would have cried out if my lips had not still been closed in that kiss, even though I could see Karya receding above me. She rushed upward as I descended, up with the sky that had somehow come detached from the earth, and the ground closed over me again.

7

Dirt poured over me, pushing me down, always down. Below my feet, the ground kept giving way, as though someone had drilled a tomb for me in the earth, and I sank as it opened up to receive me. I tried to fight against it, to claw my way up, but always the soil piled in on top of me as I fell. It filled my mouth and my eyes, so I couldn't see, or scream, or know where I was, only that I was going down, always down.

Then came a moment when I was free-falling, not sinking, and I fell onto my hands and knees in an open space, coughing and choking the dirt out of my mouth and crying, turning the dirt in my eyes into mud. It was cold, cold all around me, but dead, with no movement of the air, and silent—except for my own sputtering. The ground under my fingers felt hard: not packed hard like the floor of the barn, but hard like the earth beneath the grass, or around the roots of the trees. I could press my fingers into it, gouge out a grip for myself until my fingernails filled with it, but beyond that it resisted me.

I coughed and spit the worst of the dirt from my mouth and throat, and that's when I realized how strange my lungs felt as they moved. I felt stiff inside, as if my organs had been replaced with clockwork. My whole body, actually, felt more rigid, without being any harder to move.

What did she do to me? I thought, but there was time for that later. First I had to get out of this hole, this—wherever she had sent me. I blinked and wiped the wet soil from my eyes with the back of my hand, and tried to stand up. I stumbled over my own legs—couldn't make them work at first—but after a few false starts, I was able to stand and feel for the sides of my prison.

Almost at once, I found a wall—a wall of packed dirt, with the ragged ends of roots sticking out of it toward the top. I almost laughed with relief, but this brought back another coughing spell. When it was over, I felt as far up the wall as I could. The ceiling was beyond my reach. But it was a start. I could dig my way out, dig gradually up through the hard dirt of this wall, until I reached the surface.

I began to claw at the earth, and it gave way quickly under my fingers. I pulled out a few handfuls of it, and almost at once I reached looser earth that slid out as I dug. But more fell in to replace it. As soon as I pulled out a handful of it, the space I had cleared would fill up, and I couldn't make any progress. The space around my feet started filling up with loose dirt that I had dug out of the wall, but I could never clear even a small enough space to climb into. I stepped out of the dirt around my feet and tried to use it to raise myself up a little higher, but this didn't help me. I couldn't make a dent of any real size in the wall; any work I did was always being filled in again.

Panting, I staggered back a step. I tried to reassure myself: there was bound to be some loose earth that would fall into a hole like this, but it couldn't last forever. If anything, event-ually the whole of the ground above where I dug would fall in, and light from above would fall into my hole. Then I could climb my way out. With this certainty in my mind, I attacked the wall again, digging as fast as my arms could move. I dug and dug, and the pile of dirt around my feet grew, and even though I never seemed to be making any progress, I kept telling myself that soon there would not be any dirt left to fall in on me.

I don't know how long this lasted, but eventually I realized that I was standing waist-deep in fresh soil that I had thrown down around my own legs. I wasn't digging myself out. I was digging myself in. Panic swept over me, and a sudden fear that I would be walled in on every side. I tried to turn and step back from the wall, back into the open space, but my feet got tangled up, and I fell face-downward into the loose dirt. My hands found the hard floor of the hole a little beyond where I fell, and I scrambled forward, whimpering, until I had freed myself from my own trap.

Now I felt really, truly afraid, alone in the dark and with no way out, sealed into the earth. I began crying, like a child, moaning and wailing without shame, without anyone to hear me. Curled up on my hands and knees, my forehead pressed against the dirt, I wept, and coughed as my weeping loosened more of the dirt I hadn't been able to choke up before. I pressed my hands into my head, as though I could have contained the panic and the terror, and even my own hands still felt strange to me. This only renewed the panic. Now I couldn't even take comfort in my own body. I pulled my hands away from my head and scrambled up, still crying, and I started calling out for Molly, for anyone, anyone at all to hear me in this tomb. But my voice didn't even echo; the sounds just died as soon as they left my mouth, and even when I had screamed myself hoarse I was still alone, in the darkness.

Except that... it was not quite so dark now. For the first time, as I grew calm again and got my breathing under control, I realized I could see the piles of dirt around me, and the walls of the tunnel on either side. And the ceiling above—which was moving. The ceiling was trembling, just above and to the right of me. One small spot in the earth was stirring, and dirt was starting to fall into the hole. I caught my breath again, and started backing away, afraid of being buried under whatever might be caving in above me. Soon I had my back to the wall where I'd been digging, and just then a whole rush of dirt fell into the hole, and an opening appeared in the ceiling.

For a moment, I only held my breath, and there was silence. Then a clicking noise came from the opening, and almost at once, a shape appeared. It was the head of some animal, poking out into the chamber. It twisted back and forth, then it seemed to see me, and the whole creature crawled out into the tunnel. It flitted across the ceiling and down the wall, down onto the floor, and it sat there for a moment, looking at me.

It was the squirrel—the same squirrel I had just seen outside the basement—but now it was close enough to take in just how big it really was. It watched me in the gloom for a few seconds, then twitched and darted over to the wall, then sat still again and looked at me. Then it ran forward, then back again, then over to the opposite wall, approaching me by degrees. I couldn't hold my breath any longer, and I started gasping in huge gulps of air, but I still couldn't move. Finally the squirrel stopped, just a foot or so in front of me, and looked up at me. I could see its glossy black eyes, with a hint of a green glow in them, looking up at me, as it cocked its head this way and that, sizing me up, or maybe waiting for me to speak first.

Then it darted to one side again, and it begins to chatter—a sharp, loud sound in such close quarters. Even though I was still petrified, I remember feeling actually almost annoyed with it, and I had to bite back a laugh when I realized how ridiculous this was. But before I could decide what to do next, the squirrel's voice changed, and I begin to hear words mixed with the clicking and chirping.

"The Yakshi! The Yakshi! She has it, the Yakshi! The Yakshi has it, the Yakshi! The Yakshi, the Yakshi has it!"

It keeps leaping back and forth as it repeats this, only stopping now and again to tilt its head and look at me. Again, I feel this urge to laugh, but also to scream at it, just to shut it up. My heart's pounding against my ribs, but finally I take a deep breath and shout back.

"What? What?" I yell. "What is that? Who is the Yakshi?"

It might as well be squirrel-chattering, because the squirrel doesn't take any notice.

"The Yakshi! The Yakshi has it, the Yakshi! She has it!"

"Oh my god!" I scream. "What is that? Has what? What does she have? What do you want?"

Now I'm in a shouting match with a squirrel, because it won't shut up, and I'll be damned if I'm going to let it win.

"What is the Yakshi? What does she have? What do you want from me? Who is the Yakshi!"

"She has it; the Yakshi has it! The Yakshi has it!"

"SO WHAT," I bellow, at the top of my voice, hoarse as it is. "So what! The Yakshi has it! What do I do?"

The squirrel finally stops its infuriating rant and looks up at me again. Then it starts over again.

"Sing and dance, Watcher! Sing and dance! Sing, Watcher! Sing and dance! Sing and dance, Watcher! Before she is strong! Watcher, sing, sing and dance! Before she is strong, sing—sing and dance, Watcher!"

Then it starts running away from me, away from the wall where I'd been digging, then darting back toward me. It keeps chattering the whole time—"Sing and dance, Watcher!"—but it also keeps trying to lead me away from where I'm standing. For the first time, I realize there's no wall in the other direction. The hole I've been trying to get out of is really a tunnel, and it leads… somewhere.

I take a step forward, then I pause, and think about how ridiculous this is. Even in this terrible situation, trapped in a tunnel below the earth, I'm about to follow a talking squirrel into the darkness. But what else can I do? There's nothing—no way out—and at least this annoying rodent seems to know something. I take another step, and the squirrel pauses and looks up at me. Then it flits away down the tunnel again, still telling me to sing and dance. I make up my mind, at last, to follow, and I start walking after it.

As soon as it realizes I'm following, it runs farther ahead and disappears into the darkness ahead for a moment, then it reappears. And then a thought strikes me that probably should have occurred to me before: where's the light?

Why can I see down here, completely cut off from the sun? My eyes have adjusted to the darkness, but that only works if there's at least a little bit of light somewhere. Where is that light? Why am I not walking blind?

The squirrel disappears again, then reappears a second or so later, but not because it has come back toward me. It's actually sitting still, looking back at me, and I realize: the light is me. I've caught up to the squirrel, and I've brought the light with me. The light is me.

I look down at myself, hold up my hands. And I see the long, thin fingers, the knobby knuckles, the pointed fingernails. I look at my body, and see the elongated shape, the gray-green skin—skin that is giving off a faint, soft green glow.

Karya. Me. I am Karya; I have her body.

8

My heart starts pounding again, and I feel my breathing get rough and sharp. There's a dragging feeling in my throat, and I realize it's my voice, screaming into the darkness.

The squirrel jumps back toward me as I stagger to the right-hand wall of the tunnel to hold myself up. If I have the gray woman's body, she must have mine. She is me, up on the surface, walking around under the sun while I'm down here, living my life, and—oh, god—in my house, with my wife. With Molly, with Molly, with Molly, with Molly, oh god, no, oh no, no, no, no, no!

I'm shaking now, crying out "no, no, no!" while I clench my eyes shut, because maybe when I open them it'll be my body again, my hands, my face: not those glowing green eyes or that gray skin. But I do open them, and it's still her—Karya's body, down here in this hole. And she's up there, and doing god knows what to Molly, and how do I get back? How do I get back?

The squirrel is sitting still again, looking at me. I lunge for it, and it darts away, retreats, then sits and looks at me again.

"Where is she?" I scream at it. "Where is she? How do I get out? She has my wife! Molly! Where is she? Tell me!"

The squirrel cocks its head at me for just the tiniest moment, then it takes off running, straight past me. I try to grab at it again, but it flies past me, then scrambles up the wall of the tunnel, back into the hole it came in by. One last gray flash of its tail, and it's gone.

I rush after it, and try to leap up into the hole it left behind, to grab hold of it and climb my way out. But I can't even reach it, not even with my longer body. And almost as soon as I reach for it, dirt starts to fall through it into the tunnel again, and the hole fills up right before my eyes. In just a few seconds, it might as well have not existed.

Silence falls again: only the sound of my own panting and weeping for companionship. I stand, just looking up at where the hole used to be—where the squirrel has gone— trying to convince myself it will reappear, will show me the way out. But nothing else moves; nothing else makes a sound.

At last, I convince myself that waiting is useless. I can't stop thinking about Molly, up there with a stranger who's wearing my body, but I can't get back to her by standing in one place, looking up at the ground. The tunnel only leads one way, and that squirrel did seem to know something. I clench my teeth, and ball my pointed fingers into fists, and I turn and start walking down the tunnel, into the darkness —but I take the light with me.

I don't know how long I walked. Not too long, I think, but it was hard to feel sure without the sun, without the movement of the trees or the clouds to tell me where I was, or how the world was changing. Everything was silence, all around me. Even my feet—bare, long-toed, with too many knuckles for a human—made hardly any sound on the dirt as I walked. The light from my body never showed me anything beyond a few feet ahead; it was like the world below the earth was creating itself for me as I ventured farther and farther into it.

The first sound I heard from up ahead was the faint sound of wind, whistling and moaning in the darkness. At first I stopped, listening to make sure I wasn't imagining it, but then I started walking again, faster. Wind had to mean a way out, some kind of opening into the earth that would let in the air from outside—from the world I was trying to get back to.

As I hurried forward, it grew stronger, louder: the sound of wind in the tree branches, rattling the last few dried-up autumn leaves. But suddenly I stopped again. There was something else in the sound: a voice—the voice of someone crying in pain, or fear, or sorrow. Terror struck me again, but I couldn't let it deter me; I had to get back to the surface, to Molly. I strode on, and the sound of the wind—the moaning and weeping—grew louder, more clearly the same haunted sound. And I could hear another sound, too: a crunching and gnawing sound, like a dog chewing on a bone. A particularly loud *crunch* sparked an even louder wail of agony, and I heard a *hiss* in the distance.

But not far in the distance. Even though I couldn't see much beyond my own circle of light, I could tell I was drawing near to the source of these sounds. Soon I would be upon it—or them; I felt sure now that I was hearing more than one creature—and my mind was racing again. I could feel danger wafting toward me from down the tunnel, and I couldn't let myself hang back, but I also couldn't imagine how I would meet whatever was coming. And before I could form any kind of resolve, I saw shapes coalescing out of the darkness ahead, and I froze again.

The first thing I saw was a cage, a cage made of roots, like the roots of trees. They curved down out of the earth at the top of the tunnel and shaped themselves into an oblong sort of cocoon—a core of thick, knotted roots surrounded by a thinner, mossier web. Except that the web was being eaten away. Actually eaten: a small, black creature was clinging to the cage, gnawing away at one of the thicker bars, and it had already devoured the thinner protective covering around it.

The creature was—well, it was hard to describe, because it seemed to soak in the light and give nothing back. It seemed vaguely dog-shaped, but with spiny, almost spiky fur, which had an oily sheen to it. It had tiny, shiny black eyes, but even they didn't reflect the light from my body; they shone red, not green. It looked up as I took another step forward, and it hissed at me, then clambered back a little on the cocoon. But right away it started gnawing at the roots again, and I heard again the sound of moaning on the wind.

Then I realized what was making the sound. Inside the cocoon was a—a thing, like Karya, like me—but even less human. Her eyes were too big, and her mouth too small, and where her hands and feet should have been, her limbs only split off into many-stranded tendrils that wound themselves into the cocoon itself—that *were* the cocoon itself, I suddenly saw. The thing—the woman—was part of the cage that surrounded her, and she was moaning and wailing as the black creature outside it gnawed and tore at the roots that protected her.

I was breathing hard and fast now, and I took another step forward, feeling like I had to do something, to intervene and protect the tree-woman. As soon as I moved, she caught sight of me, and her dark, solid-colored green eyes widened.

"Watcher!" she cried out to me, and her voice was like the fluttering of the fresh spring leaves in the rain. "Watcher, sing to me! Sing your song, Watcher—save me!"

I froze again, looking into her eyes. The black creature hissed at me again, and circled even farther around the cocoon, backing away from me. I could feel anger and fear and confusion battling inside me, but the tree-woman cried out again when the creature resumed its torments.

"Watcher, save me! Sing your song; sing to me, Watcher, please!"

Her pleas ended in another shrill whistling of the wind as the black creature sank its teeth into her roots. I opened my mouth, but I didn't know what song she meant. What was I to sing? How could I save her? I wasn't the savior she was expecting, the Watcher; I only had her body. And how was I to know if any power remained in it—or in me?

But I couldn't stand by and watch her be devoured. I shut my eyes, and took a deep breath—filled my lungs with a song, any song, whatever song would come to me first.

And it came: the song I was singing the first time I saw Molly, looking up at me from the third row in that old church. It's a trivial song—almost a nonsense song—and I don't know why it came to me then. It couldn't have been less suitable to such a dark, desolate place, or such a terrifying situation, but it was what came up out of me.

If I could be small—as big as a firefly—
Where could I go, and what could I see?
If I could just glow—be my own light in the sky—
What new horizons would open to me?
Maybe I'd make an ephemeral work,
A painting that lasts just a second or two,
A piece of line art using only a twerk
Of my bright little butt, seen by just me and you.

I'd light on your finger, if I could,
And you could take me home in a jar,
Or anywhere you wanted, as long as you would
Feed me on the tiny little bits of your heart.
'Cause I can see anything from up in the air,
And there's no way to make me burn brighter,
But maybe,
Oh maybe,
Baby, Honey,
If you will just hold me, keep me, love me,
I will set your world alight with my little fire,
And you will show me what I couldn't find anywhere.

I started out soft and scratchy, and my voice sounded so strange in my ears, but even before I finished the second line, the tree-woman was starting to glow—the same green glow that was coming out of my skin. But hers kept growing, getting brighter and brighter, lighting up the whole tunnel. As I got to the end of the first verse, the roots around her, that made up her cocoon, also began to glow. Soon she seemed to be almost *made* of light. The spiny black creature was flattening down, twisting its head away from her, but it still clung to her roots. I kept singing, and my song was coursing through my head; I felt like it was burning in my mind, desperate to break free and save the tree-woman from the creature that was attacking her.

I started into the chorus, but I almost didn't get past the first few words. They nearly choked silent in my mouth when the tree-woman and her cocoon suddenly burst into flames! Green fire tore out of her, and surrounded the whole cocoon, and the black creature was engulfed. It shrieked and leaped off the cocoon of roots, rolling around and thrashing on the ground. Somehow I was able to continue my song, and the tree-woman kept burning, even when her tormentor had extinguished itself and given me one last hiss, then run off into the darkness beyond us.

I finished the chorus, and fell silent. The green fire gradually subsided, and the tree-woman faded back into a dull green glow. I watched her burn low, her eyes closed, and I saw that the roots that surrounded her were repairing themselves, slowly knitting back together into a dense web.

At last she opened her eyes and looked at me, and her soft, rippling voice called out to me from inside the cocoon.

"Watcher, thank you! You sang! You sang a new song, Watcher! You give me fire, such fire, with your song! You keep us burning, Watcher, thank you!"

I took step toward her, then hesitated. But she kept thanking me, praising me for my song, and I steeled myself to draw near to her. I came up close to her cage of roots, and I looked in through the outer shell, into her deep, glowing eyes.

"What was that?" I asked. "What was that creature? And where did the fire come from? How do I call it back? Do you know where...."

But I trailed off, because she had turned her head to look directly into my face, and her mouth had fallen open. Her features were strange to me, and I couldn't read the full range of her expression, but I could recognize—I'm sure of it—I could tell she was afraid again. And this time it was a deeper, more existential horror, not just a fear of attack or pain. Her gaze bored into me, and then she lifted up her head and began to wail again.

9

"You are not the Watcher! No, not she, not she! Lost, we are all lost! We shall go down into the earth, faceless, shapeless, voiceless! We shall go down into the earth without the song, without the fire, without the Watcher!"

My heart turned to ice, and I stumbled over my words trying to reassure the frantic tree-woman. "No, the Watcher—she sent me! She sent me here—she sent me to… to retrieve the fire. She sent me!"

But if anything, this only amplified her distress. Her cries grew higher, shriller, until I clutched my hands to my ears.

"The fire, the fire! We shall go down into the earth! The Watcher, you are not the Watcher! Oh, sing and dance for us, Watcher, sing and dance! Save us, Watcher! Make us burn, make us burn!"

I backed away from the cage, still covering my ears, and she kept crying. I tried to shout out to her, to drown out her cries so I could find answers to my questions.

"Please!" I yelled. "I can find it! I can find the fire, if you—please! Please, listen! The Watcher sent me! Where can I find it? Where? Listen!"

But she would not hear me; she only kept wailing and calling out for the Watcher to sing, and accusing me of not being the true Watcher. At last, I just had to give up. I turned away from her and kept walking down the tunnel, but her cries pursued me for a long way, wailing that we would all go down into the earth.

And I did go down. The tunnel began to slope—not much, but steadily downward. Even after the tree-woman's wailing faded away behind me, though, I didn't feel quite so alone. I could still feel the pulsing of the song in my chest—the song that had kindled the green fire and driven away the tree-woman's tormentor—and I could hear my own voice in my ears, the echoes of my song. Even if I was not the Watcher, only wearing her skin, I had sung, and I had made the fire appear. Was it possible that I might really be able to retrieve the fire, as Karya said—and whatever the fire might turn out to be? If I had caught a glimpse of it, burning in the body of the tree-woman and her cocoon, I could see why she so desperately wanted it back, but how had she lost it? Whatever had happened down here under the earth, in this dark world I had never suspected might really exist no matter how much the child in me had always longed to uncover the secrets of the trees—whatever had happened, some wrong had been done, some evil allowed to creep in. It could not be the way of things that the trees were always being devoured from below, their spirits suffering and withering. It could not.

I clenched my teeth as I thought this thought, but then, out of the darkness to my right, I started to make out the shape of another cocoon of roots, exactly like the one that protected the tree-woman I had just saved. Everything was still quiet, all around me. And the root-cage hung quiet, too, because it was empty. I drew closer to it, then took a step back, my stomach twisting inside me.

The outer mesh of roots and moss had been shredded into nothing. Only the core of tougher, thicker roots remained, and even they had been torn apart. If anything like the tree-woman had once occupied this shell, she was gone now. The ragged ends of the roots dangled above my head: just an empty, hollowed-out space where something beautiful had once lived.

The warmth of my flame that I had kindled had left me, and the darkness came swarming over me again—the cold and the darkness, and the silence. I turned away from the shreds of the root-cocoon and started back down the tunnel again. But I hadn't walked far before another ravaged bundle of roots appeared—and then another, and another. The dwelling places of the dryads—this is what I had decided they must be: tree-spirits out of old myths and legends—these dwelling places had become their tombs. Or, no, not tombs, or I would have at least seen them lying dark and silent within. *Snares, prisons*, I found myself thinking. What had once kept them safe and nourished them had, at the end, only bound them, left them vulnerable and helpless. And along had come—what? More of those black creatures to gnaw away their protections and… and… I couldn't even give myself permission to wonder how their last moments had passed. But the more of the empty cocoons I passed, the more I felt the silence and emptiness grow deeper and colder inside my own chest.

Eventually, though, I saw a light ahead: a soft, green light like my own, but not from my body. It was bright, and close, so close that I should have noticed earlier, if I hadn't been so oppressed by the darkness and the destruction around me. The ground in the tunnel started to slope downward more sharply, but the ceiling stayed level, and even the walls were widening. The light grew brighter, and all at once I realized that it was coming from a big, open space ahead. After a few more seconds, I realized the tunnel wasn't silent anymore. I had been hearing a low sound, growing up from nothing so gradually I hadn't been aware of it at first, but now it was impossible not to hear: a rippling, throbbing hum with no words in it.

I could see vague shapes ahead, framed against the green glow, and as I kept walking I could eventually see that they were more empty cages for the dryads, clustered thicker together and sending their roots down toward the floor, not just up into the ceiling. The hum was growing clearer, too, and it quickened my heart. It was the sound of many voices—dozens or more—joined together in a song that pulsed and danced as the singers layered their parts together. There was no apparent order to it; each voice was singing as it pleased, without any concern for the others, and it should have sounded awful—just noise—but instead it warmed me, made me feel strong and safe again. But throughout the song, one twisted thread kept resurfacing, jarring me back into the dread of the darkness and loneliness: a note of fear and sorrow, unable to be kept silent.

All at once, the tunnel opened out into a wide sort of cavern, full of pillars made of thick-twisted roots. They stretched from the floor to the ceiling, and from there they spread out into a tangled web of roots that formed the roof of the cavern. Each of them, at their center, held a hollowed-out space for one of the tree-spirits, but the ones nearest to me stood empty, their roots gnawed to pieces and left in tatters like what I had seen in the tunnel. Farther into the cavern, though—there, the dryads were still inhabiting their trees, and they were the ones producing the light. Each of them was glowing, just as I was, not with open flames—not burning—but with a steady, green glow that might not have meant much on its own, but all of them together washed the cavern in a gentle light.

And they were singing. It was their voices I had heard, all softly droning a song that each of them seemed to be inventing as they sang but that somehow was one song, not many. I could still hear at the edges of the song that same discordant edge, but for a moment all I could do was stand and listen, letting the song wash over me, and pass through me, and light up the darkness—somehow—even more than the glowing of their bodies inside their trees.

After a minute or two, I took a few steps more into the cavern, passing between the root-columns with the singing dryads, suspended a few feet above my head, all glowing, with their eyes closed and their limbs twisted into the roots of their trees: what they *were* inseparable from what made them. Now I could see, every time one of those notes of sadness or fear shuddered through the song, that each of them would shudder too, and pain would cross their serene faces. But peace would replace it at once, even though I felt sure, the longer I watched, that the discord was growing more frequent.

Then I saw, still far ahead of me—just a glimpse through the many intertwined pillars of roots—an even bigger, mightier column. The fibers that formed it were thicker, and its circumference was bigger, than all the other columns, and it stretched even farther up into the ceiling, which rose around it. But what was strangest about it to me—at that moment, at least—was that no spirit inhabited it. And she had not been stolen away or devoured, but had never even been. The tree did not contain a cocoon for a dryad to dwell and sing within; it was only a column of roots, standing alone at the center of a small clearing in the cavern.

I stood still, looking up at the top of the great pillar, where it disappeared up into the webbed roof of the cavern. But then my ears finally heard the first truly foreign voice amongst the song of the dryads: a lower, more guttural, more uneven sound, far ahead of me. And it wasn't singing but talking, keeping up a monologue of its own, in words that I couldn't quite hear. I started walking again, making for the sound. I had to pass by the great column of roots, but I didn't dare—for some reason, I just didn't dare—to come too close to it, but skirted around the edge of its clearing. Once I had passed it by, I started to pick up the occasional word or two that the voice in the distance was saying, and before much longer I could make out the entire one-sided conversation.

"Oh, yes, my children, won't I care for you?" it was saying. "Won't I take such care of you, just like a mother does? They won't drive us out again, oh no, no. Liars and traitors all of them, faithless. Yes, faithless, yes. We won't let them deceive us again, oh, no, my children. We've found a place, haven't we? Finally, a place of my own, where none of them can drive me away, drive me out into the cold, harsh world. Am I not a good mother to you? Such a good mother, yes. Cruel, cruel, to destroy everything I had made, yes, so cruel. But now we are home, yes, now we are safe, my children."

It never stopped talking like this, just jabbering as though it didn't know it was speaking, and it sounded like rocks and pebbles rolling and grinding against each other. Then, through the pillars of the roots, I started to catch glimpses of the source of this monologue.

It was a tall, thick-built shape, a woman's shape (like the dryads) but exaggerated. I thought—later, when I was calm—of old idols carved by ancient cultures: goddesses with unrealistically large breasts and hips. This was like that, except that the face was more defined, especially the mouth. The creature had an enormous jaw, with protruding teeth. And there was another difference, too, that I saw as I got closer to it—although I was afraid to get too close. Karya and the tree-spirits I had seen all had smooth, uniformly-shaped bodies, but this creature was made of many twisted-together shapes, like it had been fashioned out of the broken branches of trees. But it moved quickly, and its body was flexible and rippled and twisted as it walked, as though its limbs had independent life of their own.

I had been so taken up with watching this monster, and listening to its self-absorbed ramblings, that I hadn't noticed the black creatures on the pillars: more of those spiny, red-eyed monsters, gnawing at the cocoons of the dryads. They thronged the columns all around the chattering tree-monster, and the spirits they were devouring were crying out, punctuating the song in the cavern with their wails of fear and pain. Once I had seen them, I started to notice them everywhere, and I froze, looking around at all the destruction they were causing. Already they had eaten away some of the trees beyond where the tree-monster was prowling; I could see the empty, splintered chambers where the dryads had once lived. And that explained the empty cocoons at the side of the cavern where I had entered: these malicious vermin were making a circuit around the edges of the trees, slowing chewing their way inward.

All of this had barely sunk in, when I heard the tree-monster give a delighted cry.

"Oh, yes, yes! Yes, my child, come to your mother, yes! This will be our home, yes! We will never suffer again!"

I turned back to watch, even though a horrible feeling was stealing over me: dread—a dark, nameless dread, just like what I had felt that morning in the basement, and just like the night before, in the woods. And I see the tree-monster walking—more quickly than I would have thought its legs could move—over to a tree one of the spiny black creatures was eating away at. It had chewed a hole all the way through the dryad's protective cage, and now it slithered down to the ground as the tree-monster approached. It runs to the next closest tree and climbs up to begin gnawing on it, and the tree monster thrusts its hand into the opened cocoon it just abandoned.

10

The dryad inside the cocoon lets out a wail, a shriek on the wind, just like what I heard in the tunnel, but more penetrating, more terrifying. Then—and I almost turned and hid my eyes at this—the monster grabs the dryad and pulls her out of her cage. Her arms and legs and even the strands of her hair that are joined at the ends to the roots of her cocoon splinter, then tear, and she screams even louder—a more earthy, more human scream. Green fluid starts oozing out of her wounds, but she still thrashes and struggles in the giant's hand, even though it's wrapped all the way around her body.

"Oh, yes, my child," the tree-monster gurgles—and even though it's a low voice, it still somehow sounds feminine to me, like your boozy old aunt who's smoked three packs a day her whole life. "We'll be so safe here, yes."

Then it opens its mouth, and its massive jaw extends farther down. These sharp, jagged teeth appear, and the monster wraps its entire mouth around the dryad's waist. Its teeth sink into the spirit's flesh, and she screams again, and bursts into flames. But not the same controlled, targeted fire I saw when I sang my song to the dryad in the tunnel. No, the fire licks out of her at random, and flickers all over her body as she struggles, and I hear the monster give a growl of satisfaction. It sucks at the dryad, and the flames start to funnel themselves into its mouth. The dryad's cry trails off within a few seconds. Her body goes limp, except that it still twitches and writhes faintly.

The monster keeps sucking up her fire, and the dryad's body starts to twist and deform. Her face goes slack, and her features seem to sort of melt together, until only faint dents remain where her eyes and mouth had been. Her beautiful, shoot-like hair shrivels, and all traces of her feminine shape vanish; she looks more like a stick figure drawn by a child than like the other dryads still singing in their cocoons around her.

When everything that made her seem human and beautiful and real is gone, the monster relaxes its jaws and holds her at arm's length from itself.

"Oh, yes," it rumbles. "You will be so safe. I will take such good care of you, just like a good mother does, yes."

Then, up from its chest come thin green tendrils, sick-looking shoots that stretch out and wrap themselves around the poor, faceless dryad. They pull her body close to the tree-monster's chest, and they keep twining themselves all about her, and bind her to the monster. She barely moves —all the life seems gone from her—until she has almost been absorbed into the monster's body. Then I hear one last, faint moan, even though she has no mouth left to make it. And in response, several other voices moan with her, and then I see the horror this tree-monster has done.

All over her body, bound up with these shiny, diseased-looking vines, she has covered herself with the bodies of other dryads she's devoured. Half her body is made up of other tree-spirits, until you can't see where she ends and they begin. And as she binds her latest victim to herself, the others cry out in their stolen voices, and they writhe of their own accord. This is why it had seemed at first like the monster's body had such a strange life of its own: it really does—the life she's stolen from the spirits of my own trees.

Rage starts to boil in my chest, and part of me wants to scream out, to rush this demon and tear free all the trees she's taken. But I stay frozen, half hidden behind one of the pillars, trying not to breathe too loudly or give myself away, and at the same time wishing I knew how to fight back, to drive this monster from our woods. Instead I can only watch, helpless, as the Yakshi—I realize now this must be the Yakshi, who has stolen the fire from Karya—turns away from the cocoon she's just left empty and starts walking back and forth between the other trees that are under attack, and telling all the dryads what good care she'll take of them, how safe they'll be.

Then, far away to my right, I hear another voice, calling out over the rumblings of the Yakshi. "Watcher, save us! Sing and dance, Watcher!"

I look, and there, several yards away, one of the dryads has opened her eyes, and she's looking at me. Perhaps it's because two of the black gnawing creatures had gone to work eating away the protections of the two dryads on either side of her, or maybe she sensed my presence somehow. But she's looking directly at me and calling out to me, just like the dryad in the tunnel.

"Sing and dance, Watcher, sing to us! Save us!"

I open my mouth, but I don't know what to say. I glance back toward the Yakshi, but she's still rambling on to her "children" and doesn't notice. I take a step toward the dryad who was calling out to me, but then I hesitate. What song could I sing? What could be powerful enough to ignite all these spirits and drive away so many of their enemies at once? Surely I would need music of greater potency to use against the Yakshi, who had taken Karya's fire. If I once started to sing, she would notice me for sure, and I had to be able to withstand her and her claws, and her teeth, and her power.

While I was searching for the right song—or maybe just searching for the courage to act—the two dryads closest to the one who was calling to me, who were already under attack, also started urging me to sing. Again, I took a step toward them, and I opened my mouth to sing a song, any song at all; I couldn't just do nothing. But before I could, a chill of fear passed through me.

The voice of the Yakshi had gone silent. She had ended her ceaseless ranting, and it left a gap in the air that was almost palpable. I dreaded to see what this might mean, but my head turned of its own accord. So I peer out from my hiding place, and there she is, standing still across the cavern from me, sweeping the place with her eyes, turning her hideous face right and left, looking for me.

I duck back behind the pillar again, but there's no silencing the pleading of the dryads. More and more of them are picking up the cry, calling out to me to sing, to dance, to save them all. And I want to—everything inside me that I can put a name to is also screaming out to sing, to use whatever power was inside this body to send fire after these monsters, these destroyers. But what if I have exhausted my song? What if I'm outmatched, in this new body, with this new power that I don't understand, any more than I understand how to finish a song that doesn't want to be finished?

But I can't cower here forever; that's making a choice, just as much as it's a choice when I finally take a deep breath and step out from behind the pillar to face the Yakshi from across the cavern. She's already looking my way—must have followed the eyeline of all the dryads calling out to me.

"Oh yes, oh yes!" the monster roars, and she starts striding toward me. "There you are again, oh yes! But you will not escape this time, not drive me out, no!"

She moves like lightning, and at first I'm just petrified, unable to move. I stare into her empty eye sockets—windows into nothingness—and watch her jaws roll back and forth as she chortles with glee.

"My place, yes, it's my place!" she bellows. "And you have come back, have you? Come back to drive me out? I am their mother now; I am the queen!"

Already she's covered half the ground between me and her, and still I haven't even opened my mouth. My one hand still resting on the root-column beside me grips tighter and tighter, but no words will come.

But the dryads are still exhorting me. "Sing and dance, Watcher, sing and dance! Sing for us, Watcher—save us!"

I look up at the one nearest to me, and the green glow in her eyes and her skin awakens something in me: a memory, the image of the green flames dancing among the treetops, as the setting sun faded into the west. And then my anger rekindles itself, and my courage, too, and I think I know exactly what song will summon the power of the trees to defend them. I open my mouth and begin again the song I had sung in the forest that day:

> *First her eyes kindle other ladies' eyes,*
> *Then from their beams their jewels' lustres rise*

At the very first words, the face of the dryad next to me hardened. Her eyes narrowed, and her mouth shaped itself into a short, thin line. She burst into flames at once, and burned so bright I had to look away from her. All around the cavern, I saw the other dryads who remained ignite themselves. The whole chamber blazed with green light, and the Yakshi actually faltered for a moment. But she kept coming on toward me, even as I began the third line.

> *And from their jewels torches do take fire,*
> *And all is warmth, and light, and good desire.*

Then—it almost robbed me of the breath to sing— right as I sang "all is warmth, and light," the Yakshi herself burst into flame. Only it's not from herself. The dryad next to me has just unleashed a stream of green fire down onto our enemy. It engulfs the Yakshi at once, and the demon howls in pain and fury and staggers back a step. And before she can recover, all the other dryads throughout the cavern, almost in a rhythm, channel their flames together and pour them down onto the Yakshi.

It rushes in from every direction, the fire. Even the spirits who are too far away or don't have a direct line to the Yakshi send the flames from their bodies out to meet the others' in the air. They form massive, crackling bolts of flame, and they thunder toward the Yakshi, who cowers on the ground, trying to curl herself into a ball, covering her head with her hands. Her cries are terrible; they shudder my soul. But I keep singing.

Most other courts, alas! are like to hell,
Where in dark places, fire without light doth dwell;
Or but like stoves; for lust and envy get
Continual, but artificial heat.

The Yakshi screams and thrashes on the ground, and I can see her body blackening—but not really her body. It's the bodies of the dryads she's drained of their life and imprisoned into herself that are taking the worst of the damage. Whatever she is under all that stolen skin (and maybe it was nothing at all, nothing of her very own), it remains alive, if not completely unburnt. Even before I reach the last few lines of the song, she's already gaining control again, struggling back to her feet and starting to plow forward against the force of the oncoming flames.

Something deep inside me turns to ice. My voice doesn't falter, but I know I only have a few more words left before the song will be ended—before I will have no more power left to call forth the fire. The Yakshi keeps coming, even though I can see the outside of her blackening and smoking as the dryads burn her shell away.

Here zeal and love grown one all clouds digest,
And make our court an everlasting east.

As I reach the last few words, the Yakshi shudders and falters again. She curls in on herself, quaking in every limb.

But then I fall silent. Donne had more words, but I have nothing more to sing. The fire fades. The dryads burn low again, and I look down at the the scorched and blackened form of the Yakshi, huddled and still. For a moment, silence settles over the cavern.

Then the burned bodies of the dryads that cover the Yakshi fly apart. She uncurls herself from the shell they'd made for her, and she stands up again, towering over me. What's left of her is grayer, deader: older trees rotting away beneath her more recent victims. I see grubs and slimy beetles crawling across the surface of the diseased wood, and the stench of decay almost overpowers the horror of her face. Her extendable jaw has been half burned away, but already it's reforming from new and glistening vines, curling out from the remnants that remained intact. Deep within the blackness of her eye sockets, now that she's so near, I somehow see my own face reflected back to me, distorted and faint, but recognizably me. Me, my actual body, not Karya's. I don't realize it at first, but then I understand: some part of the Yakshi can see past my skin to who I really am.

"I see where you are!" yells the Yakshi. "Yes, I see you! You will not escape!"

She thrusts out one of her arms and grabs me, holds me tight by the neck. She pulls me close to her, and my struggling might as well be the rain dashing itself against the earth. I stare back into those dead, empty eyes, and I can't even muster the spirit to scream.

The Yakshi's gaze stabs through me for a moment, then she reaches up with her other hand. She buries her fingers in my back, her thumb boring into my chest with its sharp, ragged claw. Pain shoots through my entire frame, and then I do scream, but only for a half-second. The Yakshi pulls her hands apart, tearing my neck away from my shoulder. Over my own screams I hear a *crack* that echoes through the entire cavern. My body—Karya's body —gives way, and splits from shoulder to navel.

11

The scream dies in my mouth, but before I even have a chance to comprehend what's just happened, the Yakshi digs her fingers even farther into the cavity of Karya's body, and I feel something deep inside me being jerked backward. My vision blurs. The Yakshi's gruesome face fades out, and in its place I see—blurry and indistinct, like I'm looking down through the clear water of a sparkling beach—my own living room, in my own house. Molly is lying on the couch, sleeping, and I—my body, my own body—am standing over her, leaning down over her, saying something—or singing something—into her ear. But I can't hear any of the words, or anything at all. It's just a window into a different world.

And before it has even started, almost, the vision is over. I see my body being dragged away from the couch, toward my own vantage point. Another massive shock goes through me, and I hear myself scream again. But my voice cracks and shudders, then changes—becomes a different voice, a stranger's voice, but familiar. Then I pitch forward and thud onto the ground. My head smashes into one of the roots of the pillar next to me, and for a second I black out.

But it was only a second, I think. I came back to myself, coughing and shaking. I tried to pick myself up off the ground, but my arms collapsed under me. I could hear, above me, the harsh laughter of the Yakshi, and it set my brain on fire, but I couldn't turn that anger into action at first. Then my vision started to clear; my head stopped swimming. I looked up toward the source of the laughter, and my breath caught in my chest again.

The Yakshi was holding Karya in her hand. But I wasn't Karya. I was me again. I looked down at my own arms, still shaking as I tried to raise myself up off the ground. They were my own real arms, flesh and blood. And there was Karya, her body split in two down through the center, glaring back up into the Yakshi's face.

Her body was gray, with hardly any glow to it at all, but she still struggled to free herself from the Yakshi's grip. All around us, the dryads up in the trees began to wail and cry, just like the one I had met in the tunnel.

"No, the Watcher, the Watcher! We shall all go down into the earth! The fire, oh the fire! We shall go down into the earth, Watcher—down into the earth!"

The Yakshi threw back its head and laughed, and the roar of it echoed around the cavern.

"The fire, oh yes! The fire, oh yes! I have it now. We shall be safe, yes! You will not drive us out, oh no!"

Karya still writhed in the Yakshi's claws, but she spat back: "You will bring everything down into decay with you, as you always do! Burn up the fire, and then watch your house crumble!"

"Yes!" cried the Yakshi. "Yes, burn it up! For me, for me, let it burn!"

She raised her free hand that wasn't holding Karya, and a ball of fire appeared in it, spinning and flickering as she held it. She thrust the hand, and the fire, into the inside of Karya's body, and Karya gasped as it entered her. Then the Yakshi bent forward and plunged her teeth into Karya's wound, sucking the fire back out as she had done with the dryad earlier. Karya screamed again, and twisted in the Yakshi's hands, but she couldn't free herself.

I struggled up onto my feet again and hurled myself at the Yakshi. She was more than twice my height, but I seized her arm and tried to pull it away from Karya. I might as well have tried to move a tree. The Yakshi paid no attention to me, except that vines uncurled themselves from her body and twisted around me, binding me still. I could only writhe in their grip, like Karya, and watch her suffer as her fire was taken from her a second time. I dreaded the moment when her features would start to blur and her body distort into shapeless sticks, like the dryad before her, but I couldn't take my eyes off her face, either.

But eventually the Yakshi had drained all the fire back out of Karya, and then she relaxed her jaws.

"And what will you do with it?" Karya demanded of her, in a shaking voice. "You have no use for this power—only to devour and satisfy yourself."

The Yakshi threw back her head again and roared out a string of sounds I couldn't understand, but they sounded old, somehow—old and cruel. When she had finished, I heard a low rumble in the earth below our feet, and I looked down.

The ground was shifting, swirling, gathering itself into a mound. It rolled over and over itself, raising itself higher and higher above the level of the floor, separating and recombining as it changed its shape. Gradually it formed into a rough pillar, then the pillar split at its base. It was still adding more dirt to itself, and out of the pillar came arms, then hands, then fingers. Then a head rose up out of the top of the arms: a blank-faced head, with only a thin line of a mouth to give it definition. Rocks and pebbles and scattered bits of tree root stuck out from the surface of the creature, and even the dirt that formed it seemed only loosely held together. When it was complete, and the earth had grown still beneath it, it pulled its feet from the ground—first the left, then the right—separating itself from the earth that had given birth to it.

The strange golem-shape stood before the Yakshi, almost as though it was waiting for instructions. Then I felt the vine that bound me begin to loosen. All at once I was loose, and I fell four feet down onto the floor of the cavern, wheezing a little now that I could breathe freely.

But before I could catch my breath, the earth-golem seized me by the arm in this soft but unshakeable grip. It hauled me away from the Yakshi, from Karya, toward the center of the cavern where the great pillar stood. I cried out and struggled and kicked at it, but it had me, and it kept dragging me away.

"Karya!" I cried out, and I had to give up on struggling to twist my head around to see her. The Yakshi was still holding her in one hand, but she turned her head to look at me when I called her name.

"I couldn't—I'm sorry!" I called out. "Karya, I'm sorry!"

Karya watched me for a moment, with no expression in her strange, placid face. "I have not finished my work," she said at last. "You must accept what—"

But her voice was cut off. The Yakshi had sent out more of her vines to bind Karya, and they had wrapped themselves around her mouth. I tried to cry out to her again, but I felt my body being jerked upward, and it drove the wind from my lungs. The earth-golem was climbing up the pillar of roots, dragging me with it. I flopped around in its grip like a rag doll, and I lost all sense of direction for a moment.

When my eyes found Karya again, the Yakshi was striding toward us, with Karya's body bound to her back. The earth-golem climbed upward, toward the ceiling, and the Yakshi stood at the foot of the pillar, looking down into the earth below. The last thing I saw before my captor dragged me up through the roof of the chamber was Karya's eyes glimmering up at me, as the Yakshi bent over and began to dig.

The ground closed over me again, pressing in on all sides. It filled my ears and my nostrils and my mouth, no matter how I tried to keep my lips shut. I couldn't struggle; I could barely even move. I kept coughing and gagging the dirt from my throat, but more came rushing in, and all the time the earth-golem held tight to my arm, dragging me upward. I tried to look up and see how it was moving so quickly, but I could see nothing in the pitch darkness beneath the earth.

Then, all at once, light burst in upon me, and I felt myself being flung upward even faster. The back of my shoulder slammed into something hard, and I fell forward, blinking the soil out of my eyes. I recovered my sight just in time to see the earth-golem disappearing back into the hole in the earth it had made, which closed in on itself as soon as the monster had disappeared. I stared at the ground for a few seconds after it was gone, then looked up at the sky.

It was blue. It was the sky. I was outside again, above the ground, back in my own world. And I was lying on the forest floor, cushioned by the old autumn leaves and listening to the sound of the wind.

I rolled over onto my back and stared up at the sky, ignoring the ache in my shoulders and the pain in my chest as though I had been sprinting for an hour. The branches of a tall, spreading tree stretched out above me, filtering the sunlight down onto my face. They quivered and swayed in the wind, and I could have fallen asleep right there, nestled in the leaves, content just to be. But Karya's face—grave and defeated, disappearing down even farther into the earth—floated back into my mind, and my heart contracted in my chest. And then I remembered, as though returning to my own body was bringing my own memories back with it: Molly.

I rolled over onto my elbows and knees, then picked myself up, groaning a little; even a few moments of stillness had stiffened my joints. I looked around; I was standing in the clearing beneath the great walnut tree, close to the place where Molly and I had last watched the setting sun here in the forest. I took one last look up at the tree, and another at the ground where I had emerged back into the light, then turned and started walking home.

12

I closed the kitchen door behind me and stood just inside, listening. Nothing. The house was silent, except for the faint buzzing of the TV in the living room. I pulled off my boots, then crept through the kitchen and down the hallway toward the living room, almost afraid to look in, even though I kept assuring myself I knew what I would find.

And there she was, still lying where I had left her, with the blanket pulled up to her shoulders. I stood over her for a long time, just looking down at her face, but nothing had changed. After a while, I crouched down onto the floor beside her, until I could even hear the whispers of her shallow breathing.

Her face looked the same—or, at least, the same as it had for weeks now. Karya had not hurt her, or marked her, that I could tell. Not that I had really been afraid of anything, really. Not after my time in Karya's world. But gazing at Molly's sunken eyes and her hollowed cheeks, I wondered what things she had heard, with my body bent over her, whispering in my voice but with Karya's words.

What had changed inside her head, that I might never know, even if she woke? *When* she woke, I reminded myself.

Eventually, I got up from the floor and went upstairs to take a shower.

The shower washed away the dirt easily enough, and standing in the steam for twenty minutes even washed away some of the ache in my shoulders. But something still lingered that I couldn't just wash away, or shake off. I couldn't stop thinking about Karya's face, expressionless, and her last words to me, that she hadn't finished her work. I kept trying to lead myself back around to examining what I had been through, what I had seen underground, how I had been transported to a different world, in a different body.

You need to make sense of this, I told myself more than once, as I let the shower jets rain down on my shoulder blades. But as much as I tried to convince myself that what had just happened could not have happened, I knew the truth.

And I couldn't shake that last look, and those final words. What work had she left unfinished? And what had I —but I knew what work I had failed to complete.

It didn't matter, though. I had made it back, and Molly was safe, and I was with her. With her, where I belonged, not deep under the earth, fighting tree-monsters and worrying about the fate of dryads. No matter what Karya had said, how could I possibly suffer because of her defeat?

I turned off the water and dried myself off.

Molly was sitting up on the couch when I came back downstairs. She looked over as soon as I came into the room, and something flickered in her eyes, something I hadn't seen in a long time.

"Hi," she said, and she smiled—a real smile, like she used to show me.

"Hi, honey," I said, leaning down to kiss her. She tilted up her lips to mine; her kiss felt firm and alive, and it sent a thrill through my bones, as though I'd never kissed her in this life before.

"Sit down with me," she said.

"Do you need anything?"

She shook her head a little. "Just sit."

I curled up on the couch, facing her, and picked up her hand that was lying in her lap. I ran my fingers over her palm, and along the insides of her fingers, and she stretched them out a little for me to caress. Then I looked up into her eyes.

She was watching me—really watching me, not just resting her eyes in my direction. She smiled again when I looked up at her, but this one sent a quiver through my heart.

"I want to… tell you something," she said.

And I looked back into those dull blue eyes, and knew I didn't want to hear what she was about to say—knew that she was going to bring back all my fears and misery.

"Okay," I said, at last.

She took a long, slow breath. "I had a dream, just… now," said Molly. "While I was… sleeping. I dreamed you had… finished your song—the… John Donne… song. You were sitting… across the room… from me, and you were… playing it for me. I felt… so happy in the dream. So happy. I can't even… describe how it felt. It felt like it went… on forever. You played it so... many times, and it felt... so right. It was your best... best song ever. I knew it was. You knew... it was."

I nodded. "Every dream song is like that," I said. "They're always amazing."

"But this... made everything... feel new," said Molly, starting to lose her breath a little more as she got more earnest. "This was... special. It was. But then I... woke up."

She had been looking into my eyes as she told the story, but now she looked down at her hand in mine.

"It was the... worst feeling... I've had in weeks," she said. "Because I knew... it wasn't true. You hadn't fi— finished the song. You hadn't... made any progress... at all. I was so... miserable."

"It's okay," I said, and I put my hands on the back of her neck to pull her close to me—put her forehead against mine. "It's okay," I said. "I will finish it. You don't have to worry about me."

"But I do," she whispered. "I know I'm... eating you. Stealing you... who you're sup-supposed to be. This is too much. It's not just the... caretaker part. It's... seeing me like... this. Seeing me... fade out. It's killing you... just in a... different way."

"I don't care," I whispered back. "I don't care. I have you. You're better than any song I could ever write."

"But I care," said Molly. "I care. If you can't be... who you are, what's... the point? Why be with you... if you aren't you? I want... you to be you. And I'm... killing what makes... you you."

"No, no you're not," I said, shaking my head against hers. "No, you make me more myself than anything."

But she shook her head back, softly. "No," she said. "You're dying. And I... can't take it. I've... decided. I'm going... into hospice care."

"What?" I said, and I pulled away from her. "No, you said you didn't want to do that!"

"But now... I do," she said. "I shouldn't... have put it all... on you. It's not working."

"Honey, no!" I said. "How will that be better? You'll be miserable there. *I'll* be miserable there. We'll just end up watching TV all day, like we do here, except it's not our home."

"Doesn't matter," said Molly. "It won't be... on you. The stress... not on you."

"Please don't do this," I said. "Please, just think it over —sleep on it. Let's talk about it again tomorrow, okay?"

Molly shook her head again. "I just slept on it. All I do is... sleep. Call the hospice... people, okay? It... takes a couple... days to get in. You'll have... all that time to... talk me out of it."

I laughed. "I know you. Once I make that call, it's over. You won't change your mind."

Molly smiled. "No."

I took her hand again, playing with it, not looking her in the eyes. The image of dropping her off at hospice, of seeing her lying in a hospital bed, of leaving at the end of visiting hours, leaving her there by herself, surrounded by death and the dying and the dead—they started just playing themselves over and over in my mind, and I could feel my throat tightening. After a few moments, I reached around her and pulled her body close to mine—raised her legs up over my legs, so I was holding her in my lap. She let her head fall on my chest, and I held her close, feeling her ribs between my fingers.

I kissed the top of her head, and she raised it a little to look up at me. "This isn't… calling hospice," she said.

"Just… in a little bit, okay?" I said, forcing cheerfulness into my voice. "Just a little longer, like this."

She let her head fall again. "Okay."

I held her like that—quiet and still, her head warming my chest—and let the minutes drift past. I knew I should do what she wanted, and get up and make the call, but I kept telling myself *just a few more minutes… just a few more*. And then, after who knows how many times of assuring myself I'd get up in a few more minutes, I felt her body start to relax, giving those little jitters as her consciousness gave up full control of her breathing, and finally I knew she was really asleep again. I waited a long time, to make sure I wouldn't accidentally jostle her back into the waking world, then I lowered her onto the cushions and covered her with the blanket again.

I went out into the kitchen and stood at the window, gripping the edge of the sink and looking out across the field. The forest cast a long, wide shadow that stretched toward me. It reached almost to where the pieces of the barn were lying, still scattered on the grass, and it sucked up all the light around it; the grass near the house was green, waving in the breeze, but under the shadow of the trees it looked lifeless, and still. I tried to stretch my vision, to see across the distance to the heart of the forest, to feel its pulse even from my own window, but I only saw a blank wall of tree trunks instead. It had no secrets left to tell me —or no mouth to whisper them.

After a long time—my hands were stiff when I finally unclenched them from the counter ledge—I took a step back from the window. I went back into the living room, where I'd left my phone when I first went out to look at the storm damage, and I came back with it into the kitchen. I had to stare at it for a long time, long enough that I had to keep waking it up again when the screen turned off, before I could make myself do the search and dial the number I needed.

A voice on the other end picked up right away. "Red Roof Inn, this is Tricia, how may I help you?"

13

So I went out to the porch and waited for Annie to show up. It didn't take long. She got out of her car and came toward the stairs, but she stopped a few feet away because I was standing at the top, looking down at her. She looked back up at me with those wide, quivering eyes, but some of the fear had gone out of them. I found myself despising her a little less, but it still took a long time to decide how giving I was willing to be with her.

Finally, I just cut to the chase. "She'll probably be asleep the whole time you're here," I said.

She nodded. "I know."

"Don't try to wake her," I said.

"I won't."

"I just need to go for a couple hours," I said. "Just to do something... for Molly. Maybe not even that long. I just need someone here, just in case she needs something."

Annie stared up at me for a few seconds. Then: "I understand. Anything."

I couldn't lecture her all day about how little I needed her. After another few seconds of silence I jerked my head for her to follow me and turned back to the front door.

She followed me into the living room and walked around the couch to look at Molly. I saw her face go slack with the shock of seeing Molly's drawn cheekbones, but she could have time to do her grieving once I left.

"Here's her pain meds," I told her, showing them to her on the credenza, "if she wakes up and seems like she needs them. She might be hungry, and she can have yogurt, from the fridge. Don't mess around: if she's in a lot of pain or distress, call the hospital. I wrote down the number for you, right here."

I pointed to the list of numbers I'd left by the pill bottle, and she nodded. "Don't worry," she said.

"I don't worry anymore," I said. "Not about that."

Once more we stood looking at each other—nothing to say, but no way out of the conversation. Finally, I just went and knelt down by the couch, next to Molly. I ran my fingertips along her temple and watched her breathe for a few seconds, and I tried—the way I always tried, and failed —to memorize every part of her face, just in case this was the last time I saw it. Then I kissed her on the corner of her mouth, lightly. She didn't even twitch. I got up and looked over at Annie. She'd at least had the grace to look out the window, but she turned and looked at me when I stood up.

"Good luck," she said, when I didn't say anything. "We'll be right here."

I nodded. Then, after another few seconds of silence, I walked out into the kitchen and left her with Molly.

The sun was setting when I closed the kitchen door behind me. I could just see the top of its rim above the line of the treetops, and even before I had reached the eaves of the forest it had sunk down behind the trees. I walked in the shadows, and in the silence; even the breeze had gone still. The journey seemed to take forever. Every time I looked back at the house it was smaller, but the trees never seemed to get much closer, until all at once they were all I could see, stretching out to either side of me.

I stopped for a moment and looked up at them, half-expecting something to emerge, or for the trees to cluster in together and form a wall against me. But they only stood still and silent, gray and tall and impersonal. My fingertips went cold, and my heart started beating faster as I peered in through their branches, but nothing appeared to satisfy my expectations of dread. Eventually, I took another step forward. After one last pause, I walked into the trees.

The magic-hour sun should have turned everything golden, but instead the whole place felt... not dark, but colorless. The green had bled from the leaves, and even the trunks of the trees seemed grayer and less alive. The remnants of the decaying leaves on the ground had matted together after the storm, and their sodden masses had a blackened sheen over them. Usually, the trees would whisper to each other as I passed through (I always liked to think they were deciding whether I had earned their trust yet, and they could finally impart their secrets to me), but without the wind to stir their leaves, they only watched me walk up the main path through to the far side.

At last, as I was getting close to the turn off the path to mine and Molly's favorite spot, I saw a single sign of life: the big gray squirrel, sitting to one side of the path. It was sitting perfectly still, looking directly at me with its two paws held together in front of it, and it kept watching me, without moving an inch, as I passed within two feet of it and turned off the path. Then it did move—I could hear it skittering through the grass and the leaves behind me—and it followed me at a distance as I walked along the little track Molly and I had made for ourselves.

Having a companion (of sorts) only reinforced how alone we were, the only two representatives of actual life in this entire graveyard of trees. That was the word that came into my mind, then. Each of these trees was a tombstone, a lifeless monument to a living being who had had their life taken from them and now lay beneath the earth, only their shell remaining. Maybe no one but me would have noticed the difference, but the spirit of the woods had vanished, leaving only phloem and xylem and chlorophyll… and a vague, following sense of dread.

The great walnut tree was coming up ahead of me. As soon as I turned my steps toward it, I heard a scrambling behind me, and the squirrel flew past me in a flash of gray. It ran straight for the tree and climbed up the trunk until it was nearly at eye level with me. It twisted its head to watch me as I drew near, and when I was a few feet away it started darting up and down, first burrowing through the leaves around the tree's roots, then racing back up to look me in the eye again.

I knew there must be some meaning behind this, but at first I only had eyes for the huge crack in the tree, which had certainly not been there the last time I passed this way. It split the trunk almost in two, from just a few feet above the ground up through the main fork. I could see almost straight in through to the core of the trunk, it was so wide, but when I reached out my hand to explore the space inside the tree, the squirrel darted upward again, right into my face. It stared at me with its shining black eyes, inches from mine. My heart was pounding again, and I wanted to pull my hand back from the tree, but I couldn't seem to make myself move.

Then the squirrel cocked its head at me, sniffed the air, and starting chattering. "At the roots!" it squeaked. "At the roots—the Watcher is at the roots! The Watcher, at the roots! At the roots!"

My breath came back all in a rush, and I took a step back, away from the tree. The squirrel scrambled down to the ground again and placed its front paws on the nearest of the tree's roots, then ran once entirely around the tree and back to me. It looked up, its body pointed downward with its paws on the tree's roots again but its head twisted upward to stare at me.

"At the roots, at the roots!" it insisted. "The Watcher is at the roots, at the roots!"

I crouched down until my face was almost level with the squirrel's again. "How far down?" I asked it.

"The roots, the roots, the roots, the roots!" it said. "Watcher at the roots!"

It bounced from one of the roots to the other, then back again, then scrabbled in the dirt, like it was digging for a nut. But it stopped right away and went back to darting back and forth from one root to another, just where they joined the trunk of the tree. The whole time it kept reciting, "The roots, the roots! The Watcher is at the roots!"

I watched it for a long time like this, remembering how the Yakshi had dug in the ground at the foot of the pillar— the pillar that rose up through the earth to become this very tree.

"At the roots, at the roots!" cried the squirrel, and I stretched out my hands. I gripped the tree by its roots, one in either hand, and squeezed until I almost thought I could feel it throb under my fingers. The squirrel ceased its chattering and its spasms and stood still, looking at me.

Nothing happened. The forest around us hung dark and silent, just as before. The walnut tree towered over me, wounded and still, and not even hinting that it recognized my touch.

I let out a breath—I had been holding my breath, I realized—and my whole body relaxed. I looked back up into the squirrel's face. It stared back without moving, and something in its blank, animal gaze told me it had not lost faith. Then it looked down at my hands. They were still resting on the tree's roots. I looked down at them, too. Then—and I felt this in my soul, that it was right, that it was what I needed to do—I pushed with both my arms: pushed against the two roots in the opposite direction from each other.

And they moved. They moved beneath my hands; they widened out from each other, creating an opening in the earth. The ground fell away, just as it had when Karya first sent me down into the world beneath the trees. The pillar of twisted and bonded roots stood there, stretching away into the darkness below me—down, down, down, until it disappeared far below. With my hands still on the tree's roots and the heels of my boots perched at the edge of the hole, I gazed down into the darkness, but only for a moment.

I glanced back up at the squirrel. It cocked its head at me, then turned away and disappeared in a flash of gray. With my hands still using the roots for support, I lowered my left foot into the hole and found a place on the column of roots that seemed like it would support me. I let it take my weight and slowly lowered my other foot into place beside it. Then I took one last look around at the world beneath the dying sun, and began to climb down, into the earth.

14

The ground did not close in behind me this time. I climbed down carefully, one foothold at a time, with the last light of the sun to guide me—at least at first. My eyes grew accustomed to the darkness as I descended, so for a long time I didn't feel any fear at all. The webbed and knotted roots of the pillar gave me plenty of support, and before long I looked up to see that I had left the surface far behind me, with the light still twinkling in above, but smaller—more remote. The hole I had opened into the earth seemed to go on forever, and I wondered—a wild thought, but it seemed somehow plausible—if I might be able to follow it straight through to the other end of the world.

After a while, I felt a sense of greater freedom around my legs. The light had almost faded out around me, but I looked down, and I could still see enough to tell that the earth was opening up into a wider space just below. After a few more feet, I was able to pause and look around, scanning through the darkness.

I was back in the cavern, where the dryads had dwelled. They had all gone, now; their cages stood empty and ruined, and the green light they had shed was only darkness. With just the barest glimmer of the sun still illuminating the tunnel above me, I could only see a yard or two beyond my own pillar, but I stood there for a long time anyway, letting myself remember the spirits of the trees—remembering them as they had been, alive and strong and beautiful, and giving life to all that I had loved above the surface.

At last, I began to descend again. I climbed quickly down to the floor of the cavern and stood for a moment, looking into the opening that led down still further into the earth. I had not made this opening; the Yakshi had made it. There, there would be no light from the sun to guide me or comfort me; even now, I could see only the faintest pinprick of light far above the roof of the cavern. I knew nothing of what I would find—only that the Watcher was at the roots, and that the roots must lie that way. My chest tightened at the thought of disappearing myself down into that darkness, down where that monster had taken Karya, and I looked up again at the light from the surface. I could climb back up still—could walk back home to Molly, back through the woods. But the thought of passing back between those dead and empty trees, through a world whose soul had been sucked dry, sent a shiver of dread along my spine. Whatever lay below me, it couldn't be worse than the emptiness above me.

I took hold of the pillar again, and put my left foot down into the hole.

This next stage of my journey took much longer... I think. Without the light to give me a sense of direction or place, I could only guess at how quickly I descended. But it didn't feel slower than before; the roots of the pillar still gave me strong support. Their firmness and toughness gave me courage at every step downward: courage to continue, courage to keep my mind free from panic or despair. In the darkness, I found myself rehearsing the words that Karya had first spoken to me, what seemed like a lifetime ago: *What burned in me was ignited in you. You are the only one who is able.* This pronouncement comforted me. I *had* ignited what burned in Karya; I had seen the fire blaze, and drive away the darkness and evil besieging us. Something inside me had responded to her power, something I had not known existed—or, at least, not known could take such a form. If I could drive back the darkness with my own light, I should not have to fear it. I could let it cover me, wrap itself around me, enshroud all my senses for a time, and still, at last, banish it and emerge whole again.

Because I embraced the darkness—let it close in and comfort me—time almost seemed to flow together as I went farther and farther down into the earth. I truly don't know how long I climbed; I only remember what it was like when the darkness finally cleared: like coming out of a dream, or back to a home you left behind as a child and never revisited.

First, I felt a breeze on my face. Not even a breeze— just an aliveness in the air, telling me the earth was opening up below my feet. I looked down, and there, still far below, a light was shining. It didn't show me anything—not even my own hands in front of me—but I could see it in the distance all the same: a faint, blue-green light that seemed to shimmer as I looked at it.

All of a sudden, I felt starved for light—almost panicked for it. I started to climb down again, breathing fast and almost losing my grip on the roots—sliding from one hand- and foot-hold to the next with almost no fear. I kept looking down, and the light kept growing brighter, and closer. I could see my own fingers again; I could see the roots of the pillar in front of me. I could see that the light really did shimmer, or move of its own accord; it shifted its hue in subtle, hypnotic ways as I descended. It was close now; it was all around me. My own skin looked blue, where it wasn't caked with soil. And now my feet found a place to stand. I looked down at my big, solid work-boots and saw an intertwined series of roots that formed a rough, sloping sort of ledge, supporting my entire weight. I let go of the pillar with one hand and crouched down, until my head emerged into the cave below.

It was wide, so wide that I couldn't see the end of it in any direction. Unless that was the darkness at work, because even here it was still dim—dim and quiet, except for the rippling of the water. That soft, blue-green light shone up from the floor of the cavern—rock, not dirt, not like the cavern above where the dryads had sung. There, below me, three streams cut through the rock, sparkling with the reflection of—what? I realized long after that I had never seen the source of the light that shone up from the waters. The streams twisted away in three different directions from where I stood, suspended about twenty feet above the floor, and they widened out as they went, until they disappeared into the darkness. Their waters ran, slow but steady, outward from this central point, and I stared down at the surface of the nearest one, just a little to my right, for a long time, unable to take my eyes off its hypnotic motion. The faint breeze—what direction did it come from?—caressed my face, soothing all my exhaustion and fears, and I felt as though I could have stayed in that place forever.

After a long time, or maybe only a few seconds—the ceaseless tranquility of the light and the waters made it hard to tell the difference—something rustled below me, under the narrow platform of roots where I was crouching. A voice, cracked and dry and rasping, moaned, as with a dull, chronic pain it has endured but cannot accept. I started at the sound, and almost lost my footing, but I kept my grip on the pillar with one hand and saved myself from sliding off onto the floor far below.

When I had recovered, I turned and began climbing down the side of the platform, going slowly so I could find a solid foothold. It was harder than I had expected; the strands of the roots had separated, and they all went straight down, without any twisting or knotting that could have given me a solid place to support myself. After a few cautious steps, I recognized the shape they were forming: a cocoon of roots, a cage like the ones the spirits of the trees had occupied.

I climbed down the side of the cage, and soon I had descended far enough that I could look in through the gaps in the roots. At first I couldn't make anything out except for a trickle of water that seemed to be coming from inside the pillar, dripping down through the tangle of roots and vines inside the cage. Then something within stirred again, and I realized that what I had mistaken for the roots of the cocoon was actually a slim, tree-like body. It was Karya.

Her head turned as I took another step downward, and I caught a glimpse of one of her dull green eyes staring up at me.

"Karya!" I cried out to her. "Hold on!"

I was reaching the bottom of the cocoon, and I could feel the roots sloping inward, away from where my feet could find a grip on them. I twisted my head to one side, then the other, trying to find a place where the cocoon would give me a better view, or better access to Karya. Over to her right, the thickest roots offered a gap of a few inches between them, so I clambered to the left, trying to reach that point. Karya did not stir again or speak, but as I went, I was able to see more of her.

Vines and shoots twisted all around her body: diseased, slimy things, holding her still inside the cage, with her arms outstretched and her legs spread apart like roots. The same massive crack still split her body in two, from her left shoulder just below her neck almost to where her legs met. The stream of water from above her head was splashing down onto her right shoulder; I could see the water trickling its way between her bonds until it fell through the bottom of the cage to the floor, and from there outward in three directions.

"Karya, are you... how can I get you out of here?" I panted. (I was already out of breath from the effort, and from fear of falling to the rock floor below.) I was nearing the gap in the roots where I thought I might be able to reach through to her, but her silence was starting to unnerve me.

"I am glad your spirit remains undiminished," came her voice from within, still broken and faint. "She would have devoured that, too, if she thought she could. But you can do nothing for me."

"No, no, I'm here now," I babbled, as I searched for a new foothold. "Just let me… I'll get through."

"I am too weak," she said. "She has choked me out. I cannot ignite the fire, not like this. And it is beyond your reach. She has returned it to my body, and yours to yours. You can do nothing."

I found the gap I was trying to reach and thrust my arm in through the bars. My head wouldn't fit, but I could reach the vines around Karya's chest. I pulled at them, but they didn't give way at all; they actually seemed to tighten in response, and Karya moaned again as they squeezed her body.

"Why? Why would she return the fire, after she took it from you?" I asked, between tugs at different parts of her bonds.

"To imprison me here; to keep just enough life in this place to make the trees her home," Karya said. Her eyes clenched shut in pain as I pulled at some of the shoots around her arms and they cut deeper into her flesh. "Until her disease eats away at it. When her evil has spread so far that even I am no longer able to keep the forest alive, she will drain me fully and move on to seek another place. This is what her existence has been, for many years, many lifetimes of your kind."

My fingers were raw, starting to bleed. I levered myself around to reach in with my other arm and tried again to tear away the vines that bound her.

"What do you mean, 'yours to yours'? What fire do I have? Can't I use it to free you?"

Karya shook her head, then inhaled sharply as the vines around her neck constricted in response. "Your body is not suitable. You burn brightly, but I am the vehicle. This is why I sent you in my place."

"I'm sorry," I said, and I was starting to cry out of frustration, as the vines kept tightening around her the more I scrabbled at them. "I'm sorry, I couldn't... I tried, but the song wouldn't come. I—"

I broke off as Karya cried out again. The vines had pulled at her and widened the crack in her body, and she screamed aloud for the first time. I jerked back my hand, and finally admitted defeat. I couldn't free her. I clung to the side of the cage and gazed in at her, sniffing back my tears, and she stared back at me with the same fixed, unreadable expression I had seen when I first found her lying among the wreckage of the barn.

After a long silence, I slumped back between the bars, using them to take the weight off my legs and arms. I leaned my head against one of the roots and looked out across the cavern, out to where the nearest of the three streams disappeared into the darkness.

"What is this place?" I asked, after a while.

"It is the last border," said Karya. "The gateway into the earth itself."

"The earth itself?" I asked. "What about everything above this, where your dryads lived, and—what about where you sent me before? How was that not—"

"She returns!" cried Karya, cutting me off. Almost at

the same instant, the roof above us started to shake. "She has gorged herself on my trees, and returns!"

"The Yakshi?" I yell, above the rumbling sound that was filling the cavern.

"She can't resist feeding on me, though it shorten her time. Go! Up! Back to your world! Leave me here; you can do nothing!"

15

Dirt and small stones and fragments of roots were starting to fall from the ceiling. I glanced up at the opening in the ceiling that had brought me here.

"But if you have the fire—"

"No!" yelled Karya. "You cannot inhabit me again, not like this! Go!"

Still, I hesitated. The world above called to me, but I couldn't leave her. I felt this burning inside me—not the fire I had ignited when I indwelt Karya's body, but a burning of rage. How dare this creature of despair and misery enter my forest, my world, and devour it from within—steal away what was best of it, and empty it of the life I had spun into being, had loved into being? I knew I should escape, should leave Karya as she commanded me, but instead I felt my fingers digging into the roots I held in my hands.

Then, with a massive shudder, the roof of the cavern gave way. Earth and rock rained down around us, and the Yakshi thudded onto the floor.

Even at a distance of twenty or thirty feet, I could see how distorted her form had become—even more grotesque than before. So many bodies of the dryads—faceless, formless, almost more horrifying than the Yakshi herself—clustered about her, that she no longer resembled a human form, not even the caricature of a woman she had appeared to be at first.

She didn't even bother to shake the debris from herself—just looked across to Karya and grinned. I had huddled close to the cocoon for protection, but now I disentangle my legs from the roots, getting ready to do... I don't know what, but I know I'm going to fight. The Yakshi sees me, and her grin gets broader.

"Oh, yes!" she gurgles. "Oh yes, I will drain what there is of you, too, oh yes. You have returned, but you will not drive me out, oh no! Let me just get a little taste of her, and I will taste you, too, oh yes!"

She starts toward us, and already she's shooting out her diseased vines toward me, reaching for me. I scramble around, faster than I thought possible, to the other side of Karya's cocoon, putting it between me and her.

I hear the Yakshi laugh again, that horrible, guttural laugh, and I hear her footsteps thudding across the floor. I try to peer through the roots of the cage to get a glimpse of her, but Karya's body blocks my vision. It's closer to me here, her back just a few inches from the bars. I can see into the inside of her body, through the crack in her shoulder, and a sudden, wild idea strikes me.

I push my arms into the cage, around Karya. The vines that bind her tighten when I brush against them, but I'm running out of time—and so is she. I wrap my arms around Karya and feel around with my left hand until my fingers find the crack in her chest. I dig into it as deep as I can, and I hear Karya gasp—but not exactly in pain.

The Yakshi is almost upon us. I can see her now, her head appearing from around the right side of the cage. Her vines are reaching over the top of it, groping toward me. I try to thrust my fingers even deeper into Karya's chest, and I feel a tiny flicker of movement inside her. Even with the floor shaking under the Yakshi's feet, I can feel it—feel it clearly: Karya's heartbeat.

And I open my mouth, take a deep breath—and sing:

Each night I sit alone,
Drink in the fading light,
And once the day has flown,
Keep watch to see my sprite.

I wrote this song for Molly, not long after the first evening we spent together, in a bar down the street from one of my shows. I've only performed it once live before, the night I asked her to move in with me, but I used to play it to myself in my room or in my studio sometimes, whenever I needed to feel centered.

As soon as the song started, Karya's heart beat faster, and her whole body warmed. Then, almost at once, her skin starts to glow, and I hear the Yakshi's horrible laughter choke.

I look up, and the vines that had been reaching out toward me are curling back on themselves at the ends. I keep singing, and when I get to the end of the fourth line, green flames flicker into life on the surface of Karya's body.

> *As soon as she appears*
> *She's been there all along,*
> *Hiding in the thicket,*
> *And listening to my song.*

As soon as Karya starts to burn, the Yakshi howls, and the vines peel back toward her. She crouches down, just below the cage. The vines on her body, the ones that bind the dying dryads to her, are glowing green, burning her. The same with the vines binding Karya into her prison: I can feel them burning hot against my skin. Karya starts to struggle, and the vines tighten, and she screams. The flames run all over her body, but she can't do anything to direct them. But she's growing hotter, and I keep singing.

> *I sing it just for her,*
> *But also just for me.*
> *She wrote the tune and words,*
> *And I just chose the key.*

> *And though we never speak,*
> *We share it, mind to mind:*
> *A song so frail and weak*
> *That it comes back to life each time.*

All at once, Karya's whole body goes rigid. She falls silent, but only for just the barest fraction of a second.

Then she throws back her head, opens her mouth, and starts to sing: a strange, wild echo of my own song:

> *And when it's finished, I look at her.*
> *And when it's finished, she looks at me.*

And then Karya bursts into uncontrollable flames. The vines around her body are burned away instantly. But even more, fire streams out of her mouth. It shoots out through her cocoon toward the Yakshi, and into the dryads that make up the Yakshi's body. The dryads, as one, blaze into life. Their faces and their bodies return at once to their former beauty, and they begin to struggle against their bonds—which are already burning away, while the Yakshi thrashes on the ground and screams—screams to chill my blood, if I wasn't burning from the inside. The whole time, even with fire gushing out of her open mouth, Karya never stops echoing my song:

> *And it's enough to get me through the night,*
> *Enough to get me through to next time.*
> *Enough to see that canny little sprite*
> *And send her back to faerie-land with rhymes.*
> *To lodge them in her head, and know she*
> *Turns them*
> *Into*
> *Magic*
> *Spells*
> *That somehow find their way into my thoughts*
> *And re-emerge as what I thought I'd lost.*

And that's enough.
And that's enough.
It's far too much for me, and still enough.

The dryads have seized control of the Yakshi's body. They're moving her limbs against her will, dragging her howling and struggling toward the nearest of the three streams, the one that stretches out almost directly in front of Karya.

"No, oh no!" The Yakshi cries out, when she sees where they are heading. "Am I not a good mother to you? No, no! My children, my children! I'll keep you safe, yes! No, my children, no!"

Karya has exhausted her fire. Her body goes cold again, and she slumps back against the bars of her cage, into my arms. I keep singing anyway, even as the dryads drag the Yakshi into the stream.

"No, my children! Do not drive me away! Am I not a good mother? Nooooo!"

At the first splash, as the Yakshi flounders in the water and the dryads begin to drag her farther out into the stream, Karya's body goes rigid again. She stands upright in her cocoon and throws herself against the bars.

"No!" she screams. "No, my sisters, no! Wake up! Stop!"

The dryads pay her no attention. Their faces are blazing with fire and anger, and they have no thought for anything but to drown the Yakshi in the stream. Karya turns and reaches for me through the bars.

"Stop them!" she cries to me, but I'm still singing, and I can't make myself stop. I remember how the Yakshi defeated us before, when I ran out of words, and I can't stop singing—can't let her grow strong again. She has to be finished, so I keep singing, while the dryads pull her farther out, and down, down into the water.

"Noooo!" screams Karya.

She wrenches at the bars of the cage. They respond to her touch now, and twist away—but not soon enough. I'm reaching the end of my song, and the Yakshi's head is just disappearing below the surface, with one last, unearthly howl of rage and terror.

Karya leaps down to the floor and throws herself down at the edge of the stream, but all that's left of the Yakshi is a few ripples on the surface of the stream. My song ends. I fall silent. All around the cavern, the only sound that remains is the trickle of the water falling through the root-pillar into the three streams below.

"It is gone," Karya says, after a long silence.

I feel spent, utterly spent, but I climb down the side of the cage and let myself drop onto the floor below. Karya is crouching by the edge of the stream, close by the point where the dryads first dragged the Yakshi into it. I creep my way across the cavern, until I'm standing a few feet from Karya.

"It is gone," she says again. "It has returned to the earth. It is gone forever."

I don't say anything. There's nothing for me to say. I only watch her, while she stares down into the water, through its sparkling blue-and-green surface and down into its strangely impenetrable depths.

"Do not blame yourself," says Karya, and she looks up at me. "You triumphed. It is I who failed."

I open my mouth, but it's dry, so I swallow. "Isn't there anything we can do?" I ask.

Karya shakes her head, and I see the glow in her eyes dim a little.

"It is the way of things," she says, and she looks down at the water again. "I knew this day would come. I should have known it would come sooner than I hoped. I burned too brightly—made the trees too beautiful. Your love for Molly, and hers for you—you brought back into these woods what has been slowly dying, leaving your world. You gave me power, and I made much of it. I was careless, and I brought the Yakshi upon us."

My short gasp—I did my best to stifle it, but she heard anyway—brought her focus back to me.

"Yes," she said. "I forgot my place in your world, and in mine. There is no room for us now. I should have restrained my joy. I drew the Yakshi to these woods, and I failed to defeat her."

"But," and I had to lick my lips again. "But what will happen to the trees without you... without the dryads?"

"Dryads," said Karya. "You have not needed them for many years. Who now knows the difference between the spirit of one tree and another, between a collection of bark and branches and the tree itself, its true self? Only someone like you, and even you are one of the last."

"No," I croaked, shaking my head. "No, that can't be... they can't just be—just trees. You are still here. You can't just... do nothing."

Karya stood up, towering over me, and looked back up at the cocoon she had just escaped. It hung there, silent and empty as everything else that had been hers to protect.

"I will become one with my tree," she said at last, "like the spirits who have just gone down into the earth. I will intertwine my body with its body—make it strong and beautiful, for as long as the spirit is left in me. When you walk through these woods, when you look up at its branches, when you see its leaves fall, you will see the last of the old things... and you will remember us."

I looked down into the stream. Far below, through the deceptive sparkling on its surface, I felt sure I could still see a faint green glow in its depths. I took a deep breath, then stepped down into the water.

Karya reached down and seized me by the arm, almost before my feet touched the bottom.

"Be careful!" she cried. "These are no ordinary waters."

I paid no attention to her warning. I couldn't even take my eyes from the stream.

"Can't we still retrieve the fire? There's nothing we can do?"

Karya shook her head. "Do not ask me," she said. "Ask the earth."

"But what is down there?" I persisted. "Beneath the waters?"

"It is my end," said Karya, "not yours. It is not for you to go there."

"But your fire wasn't for me either," I said, looking up at her. "It was meant for you, not for me. But I used it. It burned in me, too. If I could tend the fire for you, can't I go down into the earth and bring it back for you?"

"You might not even return yourself," said Karya. "It is not a place, like this place that we stand in now. It is an end, not a destination."

I stared back down into the stream, and I thought again about returning to the surface, walking back through the forest, back to the house—back to Molly. I thought about looking up at the trees and knowing they were just trees—maybe no different to look at, but dead, empty, missing everything that had made them magical and wonderful. A picture leapt into my mind of sitting on the fallen tree, alone, watching the sun set through the trees. But the sun was just a huge, flaming ball of gas, hanging out in space, its light warped by the chemicals in our atmosphere. It wasn't a sunset anymore—not the same sunset that Molly and I had watched so many times.

Somewhere, at a great distance from me, I could hear Karya's voice, speaking to me. "Go back," she was saying. "You have driven the Yakshi from your home. Be content."

I heard these words. I heard them. But they sounded like the howling of the wind against the eaves of a house to me. I gazed down into the waters. Wasn't that still the burning of the fire, so far down in those deep blue depths? So close, in a way....

"Go back," came Karya's voice. "Go back to Molly and comfort her. I did my best for her; her last days will be easier."

My head swiveled upward. I looked deep into Karya's eyes, and I knew. I knew, deep within me.

"Finish your work," I said to her.

And I gripped her by the arm that was holding me, and I pulled her close. I pressed my lips to hers, and I felt her warmth wash over me. That same shock of heat seared through the very center of me. I didn't wait, didn't look to see my own eyes in my own face looking back at me. With her strength—her limbs now my own—I cast her off and strode out into the stream, deeper and deeper. It rose up around me—up to my hips, then up to my waist, then up to my chest, and I threw myself forward, and dove.

16

I struck out with my arms and legs—Karya's arms and legs—swimming down into the water. But almost at once, a current seized me, and dragged me downward. Strangely, the water didn't cloud my vision, or even dim the world around me; it was as though I was swimming through air, but into darkness. All light from above faded; even the blue-green sparkle on the surface of the waters had flickered out almost before the waters closed over my head. I was adrift in a dark, formless world.

Ahead, I could still see the faint green glow, far in the distance, enticing me, and the current propelled me toward it. It began to grow larger, closer—but it was still indistinct, only a glow. I tried to move toward it, but my flailing limbs seemed not to have any effect on my progress.

Then other images started to pass in front of my eyes, as clear as if I were watching them on film, and just as ephemeral. I saw Molly, looking up at me from the floor at that first show, her face somehow clearly visible even with the stage lights shining in my face. Then the image vanished, and it took something with it. It took the image from my mind itself, from my own memory. I could remember that it had happened—that I had first seen Molly looking up at me during a show—but I couldn't recall the image to mind. Her face was gone; the lights were gone; the old church was gone. Only the memory of the memory remained.

Before I could understand, or even before I could realize exactly what had happened, I saw another memory: Molly leaning across the corner of the bar to kiss me, for the first time ever, during that first evening we spent alone after one of my Chicago shows. I almost closed my eyes to kiss her, but the image flickered out, just like the first one. And once again, after it was gone I couldn't bring it back.

Then came her face looking down at me as I lay on her hotel bed, later that same night. She was smiling with a hazy sort of ecstasy—a face I would see hundreds of times in the future. Then that, too, disappeared.

After that I saw her grinning up at me as we carried her rickety old dresser up into my apartment, the day we moved in together. Then Molly in her red mermaid dress, the day we got married. Then the sight of her standing up tall and triumphant on the fallen tree, just before we sat down to watch our first sunset at the new house out by the woods. Then her face, eyes closed, with headphones on, when I let her listen to that first album I recorded in my new studio.

And they all vanished. They just pulled themselves from my head, one after the other, image after image, becoming nothing more than history—like something from the distant past, or from another life—something I'd read about in a book, but some other person had experienced.

Until, at last, I couldn't even remember Molly's face. Every memory I had of it had appeared in my mind, then fled. She was gone from me, and nothing I could do would recall her.

I spent such a long time struggling to bring her back that I lost track of how long I had been underwater. It came back to me, with a horrible hollowness in my stomach, that I was deep below the surface. How long could I hold my breath? But as soon as I had this thought, I realized: I didn't need to breathe. I wasn't breathing, but I also felt no compulsion to breathe, no fire in my lungs, no rising panic or urge to claw my way back to land. Maybe Karya's body had no need for air. Or maybe I was now in a different place—a place of neither water nor air, nor any physical reality, where the rules of my body did not apply.

I looked at the fire, still away in the distance. Only now, it was many fires. The single ball of green had separated into many, hovering like stars far above my head, not below me. Or had I lost my sense of direction? Had I confused up for down in this airless, directionless world? I looked down, thinking I might see the surface of the stream below me— the blue and green light of the cavern from overhead, now at my feet. But instead, faint in the light of the green flames above me—or were they stars?—I saw a floor of dark rock. And yawning open, growing wider as I watched—a crack in the rock, like a great mouth opening to consume me.

My heart—if it was my heart, or if I still had a heart— beat faster, and I struck out with my arms again, trying to swim upward, to stop drifting down toward that gaping maw. But I couldn't make any progress; no matter how I thrashed, I kept drifting downward. I looked up again, hoping against hope that the flames above me were growing, getting closer as I swam. Instead, I saw new shapes, silhouetted against the green light.

They blotted out the stars, ringing me on all sides. No matter where I looked, they stood, towering over me: the shadows of the trees, their leaves swaying in a breeze I longed to feel on my own skin. Then, as I watched, their shapes twisted. They sickened, decayed, shriveled in upon themselves. Their leaves fell, shadows fluttering across the flickering stars.

I felt myself weeping—tears running down my face. But at the same time, I could feel a heat burning in my chest: rage, such... impotent rage, at the death of these shadows of trees. I balled my fists up and clenched my teeth. I wanted to shut my eyes, to turn away from watching the trees slowly wither into nothingness, but I swore to myself that I would not turn away, that I would watch until there was nothing more to see.

But then, while the trees still lingered, I saw a new shadow moving between them, coalescing from their twisted shapes. It grew larger, coming toward me: the Yakshi. Even in silhouette form, I would have recognized that hateful shape anywhere. She stalked toward me, her jaws opening into somehow even greater blackness.

"NO!" I screamed, and I found that I had a voice, even in this silent world. "No, not here! I will banish you, monster!"

I tried to swim toward the Yakshi, but once again I found that my body seemed to have no effect on its surroundings. So I could only hang between the stars and the yawning crevice below, flailing my defiance at the monster who had stolen so much from me.

Then, up from the mouth in the rock below me, a voice echoes to my ears. It resounds throughout that airless space, shivering my entire body, as though I'm hearing it through my bones.

"Fire in your soul, not in your body," it says. "One only."

I look down into its bottomless depths. "Give me back what was taken!" I scream at it.

"Why?" it says. And then there is silence.

I look back up at the Yakshi, still striding toward me, but somehow not getting any closer. I struggle again to throw myself at her, to attack and drive her away, but again I'm frustrated. And then, before I can gather myself for another attempt, the Yakshi dissolves. Her shadow splits into many, uncounted shadows. They ring around me, just like the trees, and continue marching toward me. Unlike the Yakshi, these are actually getting closer, blotting out the stars from my sight. And I realize what they are: the formless, shapeless corpses of the dryads, all reaching out with their sticklike limbs, reaching out to take hold of me.

The voice from below comes again. "What will you be?"

"Give me back what was taken!" I say.

"The time has passed," says the voice.

The dryads are upon me. They seize me: many fingerless hands twisting around me, holding me still and helpless. Then they begin to dig into my flesh, to crush and contort me. Their hands—shapeless shadows though they are—seek out the crack running down through my body—Karya's body. I scream, scream for agony of body and soul. But even above my screams, I hear the voice from the earth booming out:

"How will you burn?"

The dryads reach inside me, and begin to pull, splitting me open even further. They thrust their formless limbs into me, and once more, I am pulled back into another reality.

I see my own body—see Karya, in my flesh—kneeling by the couch again, just like before. I see her speaking into Molly's ear, while Molly sleeps, and I know that next they will tear her back into her own body and cast me out. But she must finish her work—must, even if I have to remain here, in this empty world, forever. I cry out again—although my voice makes no sound—and will myself to remain, to hold onto Karya's body and leave her in possession of mine.

And then, like something filtering through a badly-tuned radio, I hear a voice: my voice, singing. It's Karya, singing from the world beyond, and the song blazes through my mind like a fire that will not be controlled. It takes control of me, and without knowing what I'm doing, I open my mouth and echo it back across the darkness:

First her eyes kindle other ladies' eyes,
Then from their beams their jewels' lustres rise,
And from their jewels torches do take fire,
And all is warmth, and light, and good desire.
Most other courts, alas, are like to hell,

Where in dark places, fire without light doth dwell;
Or but like stoves; for lust and envy get
Continual, but artificial heat.
Here zeal and love grown one all clouds digest,
And make our court an everlasting east.

As I sing the familiar words, I see the image of the living room, and of Molly, recede into the distance and disappear. I'm back in the darkness, surrounded by the ghosts of the dryads. But they are only holding me, not pulling me apart. All is stillness about me, as though the world holds its breath to hear my song. And this time, I have no fear of what will happen when I reach the end of the stanza. The song has filled me up, and I know now how it must end:

And now for you and you alone I burn;
My eyes for yours and yours engulfed in mine;
I offer up my soul to praise, to mourn,
And to consume what you will leave behind.
For light without your flame enkindles here
What guttered in the storm that quenched desire,
And all I am is all that we held dear,
Your soul my fuel, my heart's undying fire,
Your soul my fuel, my heart's undying fire,
Your soul my fuel, my heart's undying fire.

And at these words, the stars above me blaze brighter —greener. They fall from the sky toward me, gathering themselves as they descend. Finally in control of my own body, I shake myself free from the grip of the dryads. They fall away from me, into the darkness, as I sing. I strike out toward the stars, swimming up to meet them. But once again I feel myself being dragged downward, toward the crack in the earth below. I look down, and I hear the voice echo up again, but closer this time—closer, and somehow quieter, as if being spoken into my ear.

"For a time, then," it says. And then it goes silent.

The stars are rushing toward me. The mouth in the earth is opening to receive me. I fall straight down, into its depths, and it begins to close over me. I reach upward, toward the stars, and they gather themselves into a single ball, burning green, flaming at its edges. As it descends into my hand, the earth seals me up into its darkness.

17

I fell on my face in the darkness and the rain, dragging in huge gasps of breaths, with my lips against the earth. I felt alive again, somehow, like coming back from the grave. My heart was pounding against my ribs—I could feel it. And when I realized this—my heart, beating—I struggled up onto my hands and knees. I pressed my fingers into my chest, feeling what I was made of. And I was flesh, flesh and bone and blood and water, and air, going in and out of my lungs.

It was dark, pitch dark. And raining, cold and heavy on my skin. I got to my feet. I felt like I hadn't used my body in years, like I was just learning again how it moved, and I looked around, trying to remember where I was supposed to be.

The vague shapes of the trees rose up all around me. I was in the forest. Something, somewhere in my mind—some sense I had picked up from inhabiting the body of a dryad, maybe—told me I was somewhere near the walnut tree, Karya's tree. But I could only make a guess, in the darkness, with the moon hidden by the clouds. I lifted up my face to the sky, seeking some kind of light, but all I got was rain, splashing against my skin.

I let it satisfy my longing, a longing I don't think I had ever felt before, for my skin to be touched, to feel sensation—any sensation. Then I looked around again at the trees. Even in the darkness, with their faces hidden from me, they felt friendly again. I was home, and my home was mine. The sickness, the twistedness, had gone.

But I must get back to the house. Molly needed me. She needed *me*. I looked around and took a few steps to my right. Then I stopped, and retraced my steps—or thought I did, but it was all blind night around me. I stopped, and looked up at the sky again, and closed my eyes. I reached out with my hands, feeling the wind and the rain and the ground beneath my feet, and breathing in the scent of the leaves. And I knew, just knew, the way you know your way around your own home in the darkness, which was the right way.

I opened my eyes and started out again, in the same direction I had tried at first. And before I even took five steps, the night burst into flames above me. Green fire erupted before my eyes—a long, straight streak of green light stretching out in front of me, exactly in the way I had meant to go. I stood still, looking up at it, feeling my heart racing again with a joy I still can't quite comprehend, even now. I could feel the heat of the fire on my skin, piercing through the cold wind and the rain. I took a deep breath... and started to run.

Past the green flame, past the trees that flanked me on one side and the other, past the edges of the forest, I ran along the path the fire had marked out for me, until I came to my own field, and my own kitchen door. I threw myself up the stairs and in through the door, bursting in without caring whether I might wake Molly, and I raced across the kitchen, dripping rain and mud along the floor behind me.

I ran into the living room, and I stopped at the entrance. Molly was just sitting up on the couch. She froze when she saw me covered in dirt and drenched from head to foot, like a mad thing running in from the night. We stared at each other for the longest second-and-a-half of my life—just boring into each other's eyes, telling each other everything all at once. Then I ran to the couch and threw my arms around her.

She held me, mud and all, tight in her arms—her suddenly strong arms, and her sensitive fingers, digging into my back.

"You're back," she whispered into my ear as she held me. Then, again: "You're back."

I went upstairs to shower, and when I came back down to the living room, the couch was empty. A sizzling sound and a tiny *clink* of metal drifted in from the kitchen, and there was Molly, grinning at me as I came in, and standing over a griddle with two fat, gooey grilled-cheese sandwiches on it—her favorite guilty pleasure food, before she lost the ability to swallow rough foods like toasted bread.

"You're such a kid," I said, without thinking.

"So yummy!" she said, frowning her fake little wounded frown.

I stood and watched her, shoving the sandwiches to the edge of the griddle so she could get the spatula under them to flip. I couldn't believe how normal, how real, this felt, even though I had watched her get weaker and weaker, and fuzzier, over the last few months, until she could hardly hold her own spoon. But here she was: thin and pale, with the little brown freckles standing out from her translucent skin like leopard spots, but otherwise—full of life, and laughter, and awareness. It was almost like she had never been sick. But I knew that wasn't true.

"Sit down," said Molly, after I had stood there, just staring at her, for a whole minute. "They're almost done."

I pulled a chair out from the kitchen table and sat down, still watching her. After another few seconds, she lifted one of the sandwiches and peeked at the underside of it, then turned off the stove and slid the sandwiches onto a couple of plates.

"I had that dream again," she said, as she set the plates on the table and sat down across from me. "About your song."

"Uh-huh?" I said, with my mouth full of Velveeta.

"Remember, I told you? I didn't dream that I told you, did I?"

"No, you told me."

Molly stared at me while she chewed her first bite of grilled cheese. I met her eyes for a second, but she was reading my mind—she knew how to do that, somehow— so I looked down at my sandwich again and took another bite.

"It was finished," she said. "The dream was almost exactly the same. I dreamed that you finished your John Donne song, and you sang it for me. It was amazing."

"Uh-huh," I said. What could I tell her about that song, and about that dream? How could I explain Karya, and her presence here, in our house, in my body? What part of my two journeys into the earth wouldn't sound like a fantasy, like the ramblings of a worn-out, lonely, over-imaginative artist? I couldn't mar the last hours of my time with her by trying to make her understand my experience.

Molly knew I was hiding something, but she kept telling me the dream anyway. "You were sitting on the floor next to me, with your guitar, just singing. You sang the song to me, over and over. You know how dream-time works; it seemed to take no time at all, when I think back over it, but I heard that song so many times I would totally remember it if I heard it—except I can't remember it right now, is the thing."

"So, a dream," I said, forcing a flippant tone into my voice.

Molly gave a short laugh. "Sure," she said. "But this time, when I woke up…."

She lowered her sandwich in her hand to rest on her plate again and looked at me, and her eyes were wide and solemn. I paused with my hand halfway to my mouth, then lowered it, too.

"This time," she said, slowly, "*this* time, when I woke up, I knew it was true. You really have finished it… haven't you?"

I could almost hear my own heartbeat in the silence, but there was no way I would hide it from her. Not from her.

I nodded. Then took another bite of my sandwich, and chewed it up, while she just looked at me. When I swallowed, I looked up into her eyes again.

"I'll play it for you," I said.

"In a bit," said Molly.

When we had finished our food, Molly swept the plates up from the table and put them in the sink. Then she pulled a bottle of wine—one of the best Cabernets we had —from the pantry, and started uncorking it.

"Okay. Okay," she said. "I want a fucking drink. I'm not going to complain all night, but I'm so tired of not being able to have the things I like."

That should have made me feel sad, but instead a laugh just burst out of me, loud enough to fill the kitchen, and sudden. Molly grinned over her shoulder at me with gritted teeth while she tried to twist the corkscrew into the cork.

"I know I don't have long," she said, as she got the corkscrew firmly embedded and started turning it.

The laughter melted out of my face. "Molly—"

"I feel so good right now, it has to be just the eye of the storm, or something," she said. "It might be tonight. I kind of feel like it might be."

She levered up the cork, and it popped out. I had gone so tense I jumped at the sound, even though I was expecting it.

Molly tossed the cork and the corkscrew onto the counter and poured us out two big glasses.

"I don't want to talk about that all night, either," she said, carrying the glasses over to us.

She sat down, and we raised our glasses together. Molly took a long, deep draught, and I took a deep breath, and gathered my courage.

"Do you think... have you thought any more about what comes next?" I asked her. "After your dream, and... and waking up feeling so... different?"

Molly set down her glass and watched me for a few seconds. Then she nudged my glass closer to me. I took a long drink, watching her over the rim of my glass. She watched me, too, and when I put my glass back down, she reached across the table to take my hand.

"Honey... let's not talk about that, not tonight," she said. "Let's just... let's pretend it's a normal night, okay?"

I looked down into my glass and swirled the wine around in it. After a few seconds, I nodded.

"Okay," said Molly, and she leaned back in her chair and took another drink. "So... why were you all covered in mud just now?"

I gave a short laugh, and I took another drink, too—a nice, long one this time.

"I went for a walk, out in the woods," I said. "Just to think. Just to process, for a little bit. And while I was out there... I don't—I couldn't explain it. Maybe I just... made space in my mind for something else to get in, but all of sudden I was singing—singing the Eclogue, and it just started coming to me. All of it: the words, the melody, the cadence. All of it."

Molly's eyes were sparkling at me over her wine glass; she drained the rest of it to hide her eagerness. She hadn't made me feel like that in a long time: like something I had done might actually be good enough to justify her anticipation. So I did what I always do—did, to set the bar low.

"I mean, it's not really done. Not totally. But I know where it goes. I wrote a whole new verse. Not sure how long it'll take to finish the rest."

Molly threw back her head and laughed, her high, cackling laugh, like a supervillain reveling in a completely foolproof plan.

"Oh, god, I love you," she said, her shoulders still shaking as she set down her glass. She twirled the stem of the glass between her fingers for a few seconds, and I watched her lithe little fingers, feeling my pulse start to rise.

Then she looked up at me. "Can I hear it?"

"Yeah," I said. But I set my glass down, still half full, and stood up, leaning over the table. I pressed my lips to hers, and she reached up to hold onto the back of my neck. She felt warm, and strong, with her fingers in my hair and her sharp little chin digging into mine.

When she let go of me, my heart was beating faster. I felt out of breath. I looked down into her eyes, my forehead resting against hers, and I whispered, "In a bit."

18

When we had made love, and held each other for a long time, we put on our warm, fluffy bathrobes and went back down to the living room. Molly dug through our records and put on The White Album while I built a fire in the fireplace. Then she brought the glasses and the wine in from the kitchen and poured out the rest of the bottle.

"You didn't drink your share, so you get more this time," she said, her eyes daring me to argue with her as she handed me my glass. I took it and drank off a third of it in one go, and she laughed.

"Yes! My evil plan to get you drunk and take advantage of you is progressing nicely."

"Good idea for a villain character," I said, as she took a long drink herself. "Someone who cares more about the plan than the result, so they get disappointed if some parts of the plan aren't necessary, and figure out a way to work them in after it's already succeeded."

"If I had actual evil plans, I'd be that villain," said Molly. She set her glass on the mantlepiece and went to the table with her model of Howl's Moving Castle, and pulled it over toward the couch.

"Come on!" She waved me to sit down next to her. "We can still make some good progress on this tonight."

I fetched her wine glass and sat down, handing it to her. She took another drink, then set it down at one corner of the table.

"I want to get these two smokestacks finished first," she said, handing me one of them. "You were halfway through this one last time, right?"

"Right," I said, and I started sorting through the pile of blocks, looking for the right next piece.

"Okay. You take your first pass at that, and I'll fit the roof on this turret."

We worked on the model for a good two hours. Molly corrected my smokestacks—as I knew she would—and we went on to finish almost the entire roof of the castle. Only one side was left, and a few of the flimsier appendages, like the wings and the cranes.

"I'm probably not going to finish this," said Molly, after a few minutes had gone by without either of us saying anything. (I was concentrating on piecing together the lookout tower for the top, and it was tricky to fix onto the castle.)

I looked up at her. She was moving the chimney on one of the tiny houses, and she didn't seem like she was looking for a response from me.

"I'll finish it," I said, going back to the tower.

"No," said Molly. "You shouldn't."

"Don't trust me with your last masterpiece?" I said, teasing her.

"You have better things to do," she said. "I don't want you spending your time on my weird little hobbies."

She did look at me then, and grinned, and I couldn't help but smile back. She always did that to me.

After a while, my eyes started getting bleary, and fuzzy, and Molly took the pieces out of my hands and set them down.

"Time to stop," she said. "We'll just make mistakes."

We picked up the table and moved it away from the couch, and then we snuggled up together in front of the fire. Molly curled up against me and put her head on my chest, and we just sat like that, together, for a long time. I thought she might be going to sleep, and something in me started to panic, thinking this might really be the last time. But she still stirred, every now and then, and every time I squeezed her shoulder she squeezed my leg that she was hugging with her right arm.

After a while, she raised her head, and smiled up at me, and kissed me. Then she put her head back down, and I hugged her even closer.

"I love you," I said, through the lump in my throat.

Molly raised her head again, and she reached up to hold my head in both her hands.

"I love you, too," she said. "Until my very last breath."

She kissed me again, and put her head down, and I pressed my face into the back of her neck, taking long, slow breaths to hold back the tears.

I woke up a few hours later, in the same place. Molly had twisted around some time in the night, and her head was in my lap. I had just fallen asleep with the right side of my head resting on the back of the couch, and my neck felt stiff. I sat up, trying to rub the kinks out of it, then looked down at Molly.

Her breathing was smooth, even—deep, full breaths —and her face looked peaceful, but still herself, like she'd never been sick at all. Whatever Karya had done —whatever song she had sung over Molly, whether it was my song that I heard, or something else, some song from deep in the heartwood of the trees—she had brought Molly back, even if it was only for a single night.

My arm was draped over her ribs, with my hand on her back, and I could feel her shoulder blades between my thumb and fingers. She'd grown so spare, but it still felt like her, those muscles that hold the back and shoulder together. I gave her just the tiniest squeeze, and she pressed her face a little deeper into my stomach.

I watched her for a few minutes like this, then slowly, carefully, lifted her up and turned her around on the couch, still curled up into a ball. I knew she wouldn't wake up; even before she got sick, I could have executed this maneuver four out of five times without disturbing her. I laid her down with a pillow under her head, then got up.

The sun was coming in through the curtains. It was morning. I looked out through the front window for a few seconds, then looked down at Molly. She was still sleeping, and I bent down to nuzzle in between her face and her hunched shoulder to kiss her on the temple one last time before I got dressed.

I did glance at Molly once more when I came back downstairs, but after that I went into my studio. I picked up the staff paper I had scattered the day before—such a long time ago. I tidied up after my outburst, then sat down at the piano and started playing through the new lines of my song, writing it down as I went.

When I was halfway through the second line, I caught a movement at the corner of my eye. I turned, and Molly was there, hugging her robe around her.

"Don't mind me," she said. "'M still pretty sleepy. Just want to sit on the couch and listen."

I beckoned her over with one finger, and her face lit up. She scuffled across the room, and leaned down to kiss me when I raised my lips.

"Mmmm," she said. Then: "Okay, really not here. Just listening."

She went back across the room to the beat-up old couch I kept in there, and curled up on it. I smiled, and blew her another kiss, and turned back to the piano. I picked up my pencil again, then set it down. Then I looked back over my shoulder.

Molly made the "go on, go on" gesture at me with her fingertips, so I turned back and put my hands to the keys, and I started playing my song, from the very beginning.

I put everything I had into it—everything I could muster with just my voice and an old piano and the shreds of the morning still clogging my throat. I played it straight through to the end, to the very last words of the new verse, letting it speak to her, and to me. And even though it didn't have the strange, compelling power of the moment when it came to me, I felt it filling me up, telling me who I was again, and saying exactly what I had always meant it to say. When the last notes of the piano had resonated into silence, I sat for a few seconds with my fingertips on the keys, just absorbing the moment.

Then I turned around and looked at Molly. Her eyes were closed, her chest rose and fell in a slow, steady rhythm, and she was smiling. I smiled, too, and turned back to the piano.

I picked up my pencil and started in again on my notation. I played softly, just tapping on the keys enough to remind myself of the next note, and humming the words with my lips barely open. After another few minutes, I had finished the first four lines.

And then I heard a sound I'd been told I might hear one day. Molly let out a long, slow breath, almost a sigh. I heard it over the sound of the piano, and of my own voice starting in on the next line, and I turned.

She was lying still, curled up on the couch, and the smile had faded out of her face.

I buried Molly under a tree. She had never cared much what would happen to her body, and she had left it all up to me. I was going to do cremation, but after those last few days—after the way she had been brought back to life, almost, for a little while—it just seemed like the right way for her to go back into the earth. I took her to one of those new places where they put you in a small hole, curled up in the fetal position—like you're about to be born—and they plant a tree over you when they fill in the hole.

A lot of people came—not my people, but Molly's. I had always kept to myself, and never felt compelled to share her with everyone, or make our marriage about anyone but us. But everyone from her little web-dev company came, and her parents and her sister came, and a lot of her friends from college. They stood behind me, and I made a fool of myself, sobbing like a child in my father and brother's arms.

It was a fine day—a lovely day. The sun was shining, and everything was bright, and the tree they planted over her seemed so fresh and green and full of promise. I hated it, when they set it down on top of her: hated that it could put its roots into her soil and wrap them around her, to protect her and keep her safe, and go with her to whatever came next.

And then it was over. Everyone straggled away, back to their waiting cars and their day-to-day business. And then it was just me and my father and my brother, who seemed willing to hold me and stand with me all day and all night, if that's what I needed.

But then, when I turned to go, I saw one more person, standing at a distance, looking at me, and at the tree, with those wide, frightened eyes. It was Annie, waiting by her lonely little rental car, and squeezing her own fingers in her hand.

She hadn't even dared to park close to us, but there she was, as close as she felt like she could get. I gave my dad back his handkerchief.

"Wait here, just a second, okay?"

He nodded. I took a deep breath and walked over to Annie, the heels of my shoes tapping against the asphalt as I went. She saw me coming and drew herself up, and forced herself to keep her hands at her side. I kept my face like stone; if I had tried to do anything else, I would have broken down. I stopped in front of her, and she stared at me, with tears still on her face—but now she was too terrified to cry.

I watched her for a few seconds; I didn't know what to say next. Then, just like before, I couldn't think of anything better than getting straight to what I wanted to say. I took another few steps toward her, and reached out to take her by the arm.

"Do you want to see the tree?"

It was almost five by the time my dad dropped me off back at the farmhouse, after the obligatory post-funeral lunch with Molly's family. He walked me to the door, and gave me another hug.

"Are you sure you're all right here by yourself?"

I nodded. "Thanks, daddy."

He looked at me for a few seconds, then smiled, and pulled me close again.

"Don't try to be too much," he said into my ear.

"I won't," I whispered.

Then he let me go. "Okay," he said. "Call if you need anything."

I nodded, and he turned back to his car. I waved to him as he drove away, and then I unlocked the front door and went inside.

The foyer was dark, and I stood for a moment on the threshold, in the half-light from the door behind me. The house felt foreign, even though everything about it was familiar. But it was so quiet—so quiet. If I went inside, I could bring life back in with me, but it would be a different life, a new life. If I even shut the door, it would just be me, inside the house. Just me, to give it purpose, and make it a home again, not just walls and a floor and a roof.

I stood there for a long time, just breathing and listening, but finally I just shook my head a little and turned to close the door. I slipped off my shoes and turned to go through the living room into the kitchen.

But the living room was not the same, and I was not alone. There, hovering above the floor in the center of the room, stood a single massive green tongue of flame.

I halted, and my heart started to pound against my ribs. I stood looking up at the blazing figure, and it looked back at me, the face in the flames. Even through its blinding light, I could make out the figure, and the face: the unwavering, unchanging gaze of Karya.

She still bore the wound that she had received below the earth, but now it had healed into a scar, a jagged line that ran down through her body from her shoulder. And even with that mark, she looked strong, and whole, and powerful—her fire brighter and stronger than ever, filling up the room and warming me through and through, making me feel strong and new again myself.

We watched each other like that, with no words passing between us, for only a few seconds, I think—although it was hard to judge the time in that moment, as it always had been with her. I looked up at her, and she looked down at me, and for the tiniest of moments I thought I saw her smile.

Then the flame began to flicker at its edges, as though far away some wind was blowing on it. The light dimmed, and the fire dwindled. Karya's eyes blazed with one last, impenetrable flash of green, and then she faded away, and the fire with her.

About the Author

Ryan Elainska once caught a glimpse of the North Wind's back, probably because she is always blowing across the lakes of Indiana, where he lives with his wife Sally.

Sign up for Ryan's newsletter at:
ryanelainska.com/subscribe

Or connect with Ryan directly:
ryanelainska.com
twitter.com/glassblowerscat
facebook.com/ryanelainska
goodreads.com/glassblowerscat

The cover artwork for this book was designed and created by Sally Elainska using digital painting techniques. The title was set in Echelon, a font created by Ray Laramie on a Palm handheld device, with the text of the book set in Baskerville. The interior of the book was laid out by the author.

Made in the USA
Charleston, SC
02 February 2017